JANE BENNETT

PORCUPINE

Short stories

KWELA BOOKS

Kwela Books,
an imprint of NB Publishers,
40 Heerengracht, Cape Town, South Africa
PO Box 6525, Roggebaai, 8012, South Africa
http://www.kwela.com

Cover photograph: Sebastien Canaud
Cover design: Floor van Herreweghe
Typography: Nazli Jacobs
Set in Wile
Printed and bound by CTP Book Printers,
Cape Town, South Africa

First edition, first impression 2008

ISBN-10: 0-7957-0265-5
ISBN-13: 978-07957-0265-5

For you, the most truthful woman I know,

with thanks and incorrigible love

Contents

Domestic skills

When Emma had first arrived – a returnee from not-exile – a poet with orange hair had glared at her, and asked: "Why did you come back?"

Hardly a threat to the poet (there was no way in the world she was ever going to try her hand at limpid stanzas about TB wards and seropositivity), she'd been taken aback by the hostility and had simply laughed at the question. It assumed that she was anywhere.

* * *

For the first year back, the question – *why did you come back* – continued to reverberate – in her pursuit by thin men begging (even as they sold newspapers), in the eyes of upwardly mobile colleagues who warned Emma of their disappointment in her predilection for NGOs, in the accusations from the very same NGOs concerning the elitism of her interest in photographs, records, language. Even her lover occasionally sighed, and wondered aloud why she bothered to continue struggling with the meaning of making a home beneath the mountain when it was all too obvious that home-making, of any kind, was beyond her capability. "You should have stayed there; you could have eaten out every night, and I would have found someone who knew how to clean a gutter, negotiate with a gardener, do a monthly groceries shop without getting lost in Pick n Pay." Her exasperation was tinged with fondness, and fatigue, but nonetheless the question: *what are you doing here?* lay glinting beneath the resignation, queering the acknowledgement that gutter-cleaning was not all there was to the life between the two of them.

She took a job teaching computer literacy in a makeshift college for young men and women whose secondary education had not even given them access to the fact that the world was divided into time zones. Their knowledge of living between the grids and blocks of brutal laws concerning presence, identity, body and name was encyclopedic, but when it came to locating a brother, or sister, on a map beyond the country's borders, they were lost: "Is Uganda in Africa?", "Where is Baltimore? Why does my sister yell at me when I call her in Baltimore, I can hardly hear her, and she is yelling, saying, 'Why did you wake me up?'"

Emma found herself burning with anger at the sight of her students' confusion. Her colleagues – all men – told her to loosen up, relax, have a beer, after all, the young men and women she was worrying over so much could teach her more about life in the war zones than was imaginable; they'd got this far, they'd be fine.

Emma – watching how each student grappled, differently, with the slipperiness of computer mice, the intoxication of font selection, cut and paste, autocorrection – knew it was true. She was not sure that all of them would be okay, but her colleagues were probably right, some of them would be fine.

Her apprehension, and her hope, came from what had happened around her at home.

* * *

Her first days in the city were spent in a boarding house, lodging in a large cinnamon-smelling room, the next-door guests travelling sales-men with rooms full of beautiful, tall, carved walking sticks from Malawi, folded parcels of men's shirts, pure pale-blue cotton with silky kentecloth patches on the pocket. "Ghanian," said her left-hand neighbour, "but I bought them from a guy on the train." The lodge wasn't expensive, and she loved the tilting tray of fat, squashy white toast, loaded with orange marmalade, and hot tea in a dented tin teapot, which arrived like bounty every morning.

She couldn't live there forever, though, and rented a small house in a suburb far from the city centre, where the sea edge flowed out shallow and glass green across the sand and a mountain's lines ran grey, ochre, red, against the sky. Arriving at the station there at night – after her day's work in a shabby building – was a kind of balm. The train owl-hooted good night as it left her on the platform, curving with metallic determination away into the shoreline, and Emma walked slowly through the small roads to her gate with a sense of being in another country, somewhere else.

The house had two bedrooms, and Emma knew perfectly well that the possession of extra space – well roofed, painted, with a door which locked and unlocked – was not possible in a city where families of twelve often shared one or two rooms. The ethics were clear; what was not so clear was how to offer the spare room to anyone else. She solved the problem by dumping it squarely in the lap of the angels. Telling them that she understood about the extra space, knew she would need to offer it to someone else, but making it clear that they had the responsibility of finding the someone, that part she was not up to.

So it was not surprising that on her way to the station one morning, Emma was stopped by a slim woman, her head wrapped in a yellow-and-pink doek, carrying a battered handbag. The woman said, "Excuse me, madam, I am looking for a room."

Emma angled her head, nodding with raised eyebrows at the angel concerned, and asked, "Do you work around here?"

"Yes, madam," the woman clutched at the bag, "yes, I work over there, I work for that lady in the days, and in the nights – Fridays up to Tuesday – I work at the chickens."

"At the chickens?" asked Emma. "What chickens?"

"At the chickens, madam," the woman looked at her, "the chickens in the Shoprite, I clean up behind the chickens. In the kitchen."

Emma's mind snapped into focus. "You work at Nando's?"

"Yes, Nando's, at the chickens. Nando's. I am the cleaner, weekends and Mondays. Not after Tuesday night. Those nights, I have no work. I need a place to stay, I was working in Retreat, but now it is different. I am all the time here, and I need a place."

The connections were all obvious, and Emma said carefully, "Well, I think maybe I know how to help. I'm on my way to work now, but I'll be back home," pointing back behind her, "after six. What are your plans for today? Can you come and see me in my house? Would tomorrow be better?"

"I can come. Tomorrow morning I can come."

They smiled at each other, wariness and expectation in the gaze between them.

"I didn't ask," Emma realised, a little shocked at her own rudeness, "I'm sorry, sis', I didn't ask your name?"

"At the chickens, they are calling me Wendy," the woman responded, "but my name is Nontobeko. I come from another place. I don't think you know it. I'm not living in Cape Town for so long, maybe ten years. I came with my brother."

"I'm Emma. I was living in America, and then I came here. But I am from here; not Cape Town, but from South Africa. Well, I think I am from here."

The woman wrote down Emma's address on the back of an old advertisement for a furnishing store, and the next morning found the two of them sitting in Emma's small front room, exploring the terrain.

Emma's conditions were clear: no need for rent, no men overnight whom she would encounter brushing their teeth at six am, no repugnance should Nontobeko encounter her own women lovers, shared household cleaning.

Nontobeko didn't point out the double standard of Emma's rules about sexuality, but she did have some conditions of her own: inside doors must be locked when they both went to work, her three-year-old daughter would sometimes come to stay on weekends, she didn't like people who were loud or swore, cleaning could be shared, but no shared ironing or washing (she wanted to do her own). And no messy dogs; she didn't like dogs.

They decided to write down what they had agreed about sharing a home, and to give the experiment a go for six months. After six months, said Emma, they would talk again and decide if they wanted to continue living together, if it was working.

Despite the angled awkward imbalance of the thing (Emma with one job, one language and the lease; Nontobeko with two jobs, two-and-a-half languages, a guest – and not – in the house), everything ran smoothly. Both women were private. Nontobeko took to singing tunes by Whitney Houston quietly in the mornings as she made tea before going to her char job, tunes that Emma found herself humming as she stepped onto the train towards her students and their wrestles with the screen.

* * *

The day Emma returned to the house to find it ravaged was a Tuesday. She and Nontobeko had left together that morning, but it was a late-returning day for Emma – meetings after classes, an extra session with a group of students who wanted to learn how to use a data-processing package, a long, addled conversation with a colleague about his desire to undertake more postgraduate study on globalisation. The sight that faced her as she came through the house gate was senseless – a dark space where the front door should have been, cracked planks jabbing outwards.

Emma suck-choked on her breath, and looked wildly round, yelling, "Nontobeko? Nontobeko?"

Her blood racing with terror, she pushed her way past a door that had clearly been hacked open (an axe?) and burst into the hallway.

Complete chaos met her: the bookcase toppled over, smashed plates all over the floor, splinters and fragments everywhere. Nontobeko's bedroom door crushed inwards and from the hallway she could see the iron corner of Nontobeko's bedstead upended, like a strange sculpture. On the walls around her, thick crimson spray paint sputtered into jangled letters: *Fok jou moer . . . Poes . . . Ons gaan julle naai . . . Vat hom, die sex is lekker*.

Emma shoved her way into Nontobeko's room. She didn't know

what she wanted to see, or not see, and only when she grasped that there was no Nontobeko inside, gashed or sobbing, did the depth of her panic punch up at her throat.

She knew she should call the police, call a friend, but all she wanted to do was find Nontobeko.

Leaving the house exactly as it was, Emma ran back out into the street. Her first thought was Nando's, but when she got there and asked for "Nontobeko . . . Wendy . . ." a huge woman with flat eyes just shooed her away: "Wendy? No, Wendy's weekends. I have no idea, she lives somewhere here with some lesbian, I have nothing to know about what such a woman is doing on a Tuesday, my business is here."

Feeling as though she was in a tornado, Emma returned to the dismembered house.

* * *

It took five hours for the police to come – no moving anything, finger-prints would have to be taken next morning, they advised she didn't stay there that night, no ma'am, was there somewhere she could stay, a friend, she should call a friend, and find somewhere to sleep.

She told them nothing about Nontobeko, just explained she lived with another woman – no, she didn't know where she was, yes, she would make arrangements to find shelter elsewhere that night, maybe for a couple of nights.

* * *

It was after midnight before the policemen left. Emma knew she could not remain alone surrounded by the gawping slogans, the gaping front door, the blank of Nontobeko.

She pulled some clothes out of her cupboard (she could see that some sweaters and a whole shelf of shirts had gone), picked her way over the floor-mess into the bathroom and retrieved toothpaste, a toothbrush and a cake of soap, and stuffed them into her work rucksack. She found a large sheet of paper, and wrote on it: *Nontobeko – our home has been attacked. I looked everywhere for you, and I'm worried. I can't stay here tonight. I don't know where I'm going, but the words on the wall are frightening me. I will come back here tomorrow. The police are coming again. If you get this, please leave me a message to say where I can find you. I will come and look for you at your work. I'm sorry. Emma.*

She stuck the paper on the remains of the front door, and left the porch light on, so that if Nontobeko did – by some miracle – arrive, she would immediately find someone speaking to her. The glow of the little light exacerbated the vulnerability of the house, but Emma didn't know how to heal that.

She walked along the pavement, slow and fuzzy, only half-embodied in the spill of the streetlights and the grey thrall of shuttered night, the muted drum of the sea pulling her towards the beach. She knew that the dunes running alongside the shoreline were dangerous; wild men were said to live among the scrub and bushes, pulling life into themselves through the necks of small brandy bottles. It didn't seem to matter much.

She found herself taking off her shoes, sinking her feet into the smooth, cold sand, walking along the half-silver of the slow waves, furling and unfurling. There was no moon, but enough strange light from the sky to illuminate the shape of her feet and the quiet curl of the shoreline ahead. She felt lost, between human and animal, a body without a body.

"Hallo, Emma," said a low voice. Almost not a voice.

Emma turned her head, and could – barely – make out a small male figure, a dark lump to her left, sitting on a rock. She stopped. "Jackson?" she ventured, her voice sounding thin and hollow against the sea-blur. "Jackson? Is that you?"

"Mmm," came the voice. "Who did you think it was? Come closer. I can hardly see you."

Emma moved her way up the sand, until she was almost on top of the rock, peering and holding out her arm. "It *is* you! And you have clothes on!"

The man laughed. "It's true. I do. Where are you going? It's dark out here."

The last time Jackson and Emma had had a similar conversation, she had been walking briskly up a New York street – towards a seminar room – and he had been sitting on top of a dumpster, ashy with dust, but cheerful. They had been delighted to see each other. Emma had tucked herself down onto the pavement and they had chatted for over an hour, catching up, comparing notes on incarceration, doctors, mothers and what next.

They had first met while both captured by the New York State Psychiatric Hospital, locked into a ward with long yellow walls and a set of tall, filthy plants, their leaves turned against the ninth-floor windows. Emma had been caught after a foolish, if desperate, act of destruction. She had been naïve and outwitted. Jackson had been much more savvy about the whole thing. He had made a deliberate decision and his story inspired everyone: "My mother said, 'You crazy, you are just a crazy boy, and I'm not having you any more. Out of my house you are going, and I do not want to see you again, not your face, your head, your feet. It's been thirty-two years and my duty is over, you are out.'"

Jackson had left, accompanied by no more than the clothes on his back, and had very quickly realised the precarious state of things: no home, no money, no mother.

"So, I thought, and I pondered, and I came up with a plan. I took off my clothes. I just started taking them off, outside the Chinese food. I started with my shirt, and then I did the vest and the socks, and by then people were staring, so I sang a little bit to keep myself going. I am not much of a one for people staring, but I thought this is something I have to do, so I kept going. I put the socks and the shirt and vest in a pile, neat-like, and by the time I was getting to the belt buckle, there was shouting, and with the pants, I was on my way.

"People tried to persuade me to get dressed, 'Come on, man, what is wrong with you . . .', but I just closed my ears and thought of my mother. I sat down naked, and sometimes stood up, just to show I

19

really was not a man with clothes on, and I kept on singing and humming, and it was not long, not long at all. A car came, lights, two cars, and they picked up my clothes, told me to get in. They weren't rude or anything. You know how these people can be. I'm six foot three, I'm a black man, I was thinking they would be rude, but no, not so much, and then I was here. I've been here for three weeks; the food could be better, but I like the TV, my mother always shouted: 'Turn off the TV, boy, I've got a headache.'"

Jackson had still been locked in when Emma had been given release papers, and fraternisation between those inside and those outside was strictly prohibited. So the re-encounter in the New York streets had been a delight. After their conversation, they had wandered together into a doughnut shop, purchased large coffees and chocolate-covered sweetness, and waved goodbye with the solidarity of conspirators. They were family, it wasn't necessary to share blood, homes, language; kin will know kin.

"How did you get here?" asked Emma, now very far from any New York street. "I am so glad to see you."

"I've become a traveller," answered Jackson, coughing a little. "The city was okay, but it bugged me having no home. And when it was winter, the clothes thing, I didn't like it any more. So, I've been moving. I visit. Stay a while here, a while there. I find a home like that. It can be tiring, but it works out better even than the hospital. I didn't mind the hospital, but how can you call the locking up a home? I don't think that's right, locking up."

20

"Well," said Emma, "I sure wouldn't have stayed if they hadn't locked me up. So, I guess that was the point. Have you come to visit me?" She looked hopefully into his face.

He smiled at her, showing his teeth. "No, man. It's just tonight. I'm sorry, I'm on my way to another friend. I met her after you left, she was sad, a lost baby, drugs and drugs. Before I died, we talked, I showed her some ways of looking again. She introduced me to a church group she belonged to and they often gave us stuff, a lot of it was rubbish, but she liked them."

"Jackson," Emma touched the rock, "when did you die?"

"I can't remember." Jackson puzzled a bit. "It was after I tried seeing my mother again. I always wanted to see her, and it was after the last time I tried. It just didn't work. She thought I was too crazy, too outside. I don't know too much about what happened after that. I know I drank a lot that night, and you know I never drank. I got into a fight down by the piers. I remember missing my friends. It was September. It was still light at eight o'clock at night. I remember looking at New Jersey over the river, and wanting to do something different – travel, make connections – that's all."

"New Jersey?" Emma scoffed. "You thought New Jersey was travel?"

Jackson laughed and his hand pulled at a lock of her hair. "You know, girl," he said, "you are such a New Yorker, you are so superior. What's wrong with New Jersey?"

"Yeah, yeah . . ." Emma stayed still.

They sat looking out over the sea as the horizon slowly began to glisten and inconspicuous streaks of pink and yellow alluded to the need to acknowledge that the tide was turning, a day was coming.

"I must go," she said, "my house was burgled last night and I couldn't find my housemate. Thanks, Jackson."

He rubbed her shoulders, roughly. "Don't be too mad," he said. "I'll be back."

* * *

The streets were beginning to awaken as Emma walked home. She felt drained, but alert; oversensitive to colour and language.

Nontobeko was sitting in front of the gate with two women beside her, their legs stretched out comfortably into the road, all holding mugs of tea. The three of them looked up at her as she approached. "Where have you been, Emma?" called Nontobeko. "Where did you go?"

"Where did *you* go? Nontobeko, did you see the house? I looked everywhere for you? Were you here?" Emma burst into tears.

Nontobeko stood up. "Hey, sorry, these are my friends: this is Lindi, this is Susan. I was staying with Susan yesterday. I went after work. I came here this morning."

Nontobeko spoke calmly, she looked unhurried, and as though her skirt was ironed. She looked peaceably at Emma.

Emma felt flustered, out of kilter. "I'm pleased to meet you, Lindi, Susan, I'm Emma. But, sis', have you looked at the house? It's wrecked, it's all bashed in, the doors, and there are horrible words on the walls, I was so scared you had been hurt."

"No, I am not hurt." Nontobeko sat down again. "We are having tea, and I can get you some. The water, it is just now hot."

Emma plopped down onto the pavement. She felt winded.

"The house, Emma," Nontobeko continued, "the house, it is just walls. It is doors, and I have a friend, he will fix the doors. You must get new paint. We must clean." She looked fiercely at Emma, as though she might be too frail a reed to wield a scrubbing brush. "This is our home. We are living here. Stupid people are not taking it away, they can't take it away. It is nothing, this . . ." Nontobeko waved a dismissive hand backwards towards the ex-front door. "Last week, my friend's house, it was burned. Fifteen minutes, it was gone."

There was a long pause.

The four of them stayed sitting, relaxed, by the gate, waiting for the fingerprint people to search for the traces of would-be home-wreckers. There would be no traces of the assailants to be found, Emma knew, but outside in the sunshine she felt suddenly astonishingly peaceful, a settling low in her stomach. It was clear that all evidence of frenzy and solipsism was irrelevant. She couldn't follow all of the conversation between Nontobeko and her friends, she would have to borrow a ladder to lap new colour over the spray paint, there was perhaps a problem with her cleaning skills and Jackson was on his way to visit someone else.

She, however, was home.

Crucifix

In the section labelled "Craft" the prizewinner came from KwaZulu-Natal. It was called *Women and AIDS* and the designer had beaded a crucifix shape – blue, silver, red – with a small black head and two arms stiff as toothpicks. Someone the newspapers called a mining magnate had sponsored prizes for the best contemporary works of national art, which, she saw, included a set of long silver worms coming out of a wall, a blown glass bauble-pillar, called *African Queen*, and a fat, rubbery pink woman, tattooed in a too small bikini.

"We don't really look like that, do we?" asked a woman standing next to her, skewered by the pink lady.

"We don't," she answered, looking at the stranger's sleek outfit and brown arms. "I'm sure we don't."

The only thing she really liked was also in the "Craft" category. It had been made by a group of women in Hillbrow out of scraps of found cloth, plastic and paperclips. It said: *Stop burrying childs in the garbage*, showing a large brown dog pulling a stick baby out of a rubbish bin. Damn right, she thought, some direct instructions.

The stick baby was flanked, on bright red cloth, with passionate injunctions to pray and a square of people playing soccer; open black bodies dressed in red caps against a brilliant green. It made sense to her, the urban bricolage of what was thrown to the winds: childs, women, a football. But it was the crucifix that had won the prize.

A few months beforehand she had been asked to give a speech. The request had been vague: she was please to talk about rape.

Rather bemused, but loath to offend, she'd sent an e-mail requesting clarification: Anything about rape? Who was the audience? Who were the other speakers? What was it she, in particular, was supposed to know?

A response was returned: *We are co-organising the conference with the Department of Religious Studies and the Centre for Interfaith Community. They are keen to integrate research on gender-based violence into their work, and we are expecting a lot of faith-based people. So, you are free to discuss any aspect you like, but don't get too theoretical or academic. Thank you for your willingness to participate.*

Gender-based violence. Faith-based people. A lot of bases around and no theory or academia.

As she drove to the conference venue, she was deeply unsure of what she was going to say, juggling openings and orientations in her mind until she felt like a scrambled egg. Things did not improve. As she entered the conference room, a large gentleman (representing the National Machinery on gender) was explaining that it was time for an examination of the "alternatives" to rape. His argument seemed to be that forcing people to have sex was the result of frustrated egos and thin wallets. Rape, he acknowledged, was no way to go on, but what were the alternatives.

A question period immediately followed this plea. From the middle of a row an earnest young woman's voice rose to a crescendo, quoting Old Testament lines – the wrath of God when people failed to follow His desert paths. In front of her a colleague twisted her long dark hair into tangled pretzels, jiggling her whole body with irritation as the voice litanied through drugs, the price of good education, the fascination of the youth with television, the gluttony of malls, and concluded with the suggestion that rape, nasty as it was, must be understood as one of the revenges of the Lord, only natural in the face of such blatant disobediences. She felt the bittersweet spurt of culture shock at the back of her throat.

She had been next at the podium. Introduced as, "Dr X, well known for her work, etcetera."

Her work, etcetera? She paused, searching with poor vision, for revenge-lady. By counting rows she found her – a plump, curly-haired adolescent, leaning forward, ready pen in hand.

She began by saying that she very much disliked being the embodied site of the Lord's revenge, it would have been better had He revenged himself upon the rapist. Having begun without innocence she carried on recklessly. The end came where she decided to take on the crucifix itself. Speaking of Christianity as a faith that considered pain as central to salvation (Christians all wore replicas of a torture instrument round their necks), she wondered if one could replace the broken Jesus man-body with the angled wreck of a just-raped woman? Was she, too, destined for worship, spiritual salience beyond par, resurrection? And if she replaced the Jesus, what (who?) replaced the thick, terrible, cross? Bore thinking about. Perhaps.

She sat down, surrounded by silence. The chair of the session stared at her and then took the podium microphone, asking for, "Questions of clarity, or comments, anything . . ."

Revenge-lady sprang to her feet, protesting that she hadn't at all meant to say people who were raped were actually the Lord's target, but in an evil world . . . She shrugged helplessly.

An imam, seated in the front row, audibly muttered, "Oh, shut up!", but otherwise there was complete quiet and the chair was compelled to suggest another tea break.

Feeling embarrassed, she slid up the auditorium steps towards a cup of coffee. A friendly woman pouring the hot water, having no idea what she'd just said, smiled at her, asking, "How's it going? I thought yous already had a tea break, did one of the speakers not show?"

She shook her head, and headed for the hot summer air and the jacaranda tree outside.

"Dr X?"

A tall, gaunt-faced man stood in front of her. He had a dark beard, shaven against his cheekbones, but not around his chin.

"Dr X, I was just inside," he pointed at the auditorium. "I heard your comments. Very interesting. I would like to tell you a story. May we sit down?"

She gestured towards the jacaranda tree and smiled. "I'd prefer to be outside," she said.

Grass beneath a jacaranda tree is an impossibility, so they dragged pale plastic chairs awkwardly from the verandah circling the auditorium into the feathered shade of the tree.

He said nothing while they settled themselves, then he began. "A long time ago my father was called a rapist. He was accused of having made a very young woman pregnant. It was said that she agreed, but there was doubt – a great light in her eyes, a vast presence, promises that seemed highly unrealistic. My father was accused of never paying her any support; another man had to marry her to prevent the shame. Although no one said anything I always knew who he was though, and when I was as young as twelve, I ran away, looking for him, talking about him, especially to the older men whom I thought might recall him.

"My mother was desperate to find me that day, ran all over the city. I was surprised by her panic. It was then that I thought it might be true – she hadn't really known him, was certainly not convinced he had safety in mind. What had he actually said to her so that I could be born? I was disturbed by their seeming estrangement. I vowed that I, for one, would try for something different."

She sat still, the coffee in her hand pulling away from the edges of the cup into a cold beige.

He stretched out his long legs and smiled at her. "It didn't turn out anything like I'd expected and I'll spare you the details. I spent the most important years of my life with a group of men. I wanted to try another way; living without the mess of tiny rooms, women and men, landlords, chores, sex in the dark, stuck, afraid of the next attack . . .

"The way it ended was a nightmare. First a nightmare and then something else. When I came back to show my men friends that things were okay, the one thing that really made them believe it was me was this . . ."

She gasped. He had pulled aside a fold of cloth and exposed a long, pear-shaped slice wound, running from just beneath his ribcage to the top of his thigh. The wound was a world deep, crimson with blood and excavated muscle, unsutured, dank.

"It has never healed," he said. "Everything else, even the memory of that time, the smells, my mother's eyes, it's all covered over, made different. But this – it stays, it doesn't close, it's been there longer than I know."

She held onto the thin plastic of her seat and concentrated on the purple of the tree flowers on the ground around their feet.

"I have a question."

"You have a question?" He raised his eyebrows, gently, without expectation.

"That wound. From what I have heard, a soldier made that wound. While you were there, hanging. Is that right? I'm asking because you know what that wound looks like. You are a woman with that wound. Are you a woman? Who made that wound? The soldier, or your father? What story are you telling me?"

The man sighed. "It doesn't matter, you know, who made it. You will think it matters, but I am the one who carries it. Isn't that what you always advocate: the body of the wounded carries the authority? It's no different with me. It doesn't matter to me whether it was him, or the soldier, or him-in-the-soldier or the devil itself. It only matters that you can recognise what happened to you in me."

She shook herself. It was getting either sacrilegious or fundamentalist. "I'm not a Christian," she said. "Too much our-father-who-art for me. Too much subservience required. Sins all the time. Women and gay people anathema. I can't just sit here, listening to you, as though we share that thing, that X of wood and murder; mine a man, yours your father or the devil or me-the-sinner. What kind of invitation is that? How can you be here?"

He picked up a long jacaranda frond and ran his fingers through the minute green leaves, combing it. He lowered his head and then put his hand carefully onto her arm. "Dr X," he placed the frond in her lap, "that was exactly the invitation you asked for. That's exactly the one. Never invoke a god's experience if you're not serious."

She chuckled. The morning had turned out much better than she'd thought possible. She stroked the fern-like jacaranda leaf. "Bitten off more than I can chew." She grinned at the man. "Been put in my place, I think. I should stick to statistics and narratives about secondary victimisation in the courtroom."

The man stood up and held out his hand to her. They walked together back into the building, the cloth of his tunic and her long kaftan folding side by side across their legs.

He turned a corner, was gone. Dr X remained, stymied, in front of the conference posters – *Rape and Religion: A Debate Across Divides?* – surreptitiously touching the space between her ribcage and her thigh. As smooth as ever. The wound in the other place.

Extreme motherhood

He did not trust his relationship to history. As he sat in his armchair, reading about the way in which the land of cattle had been recast into provinces, it seemed as though the words would score themselves permanently into his eyes: "Xolilizwe Sigcawu . . . direct descendant of Hintsa, Sarhili, Sigcawu, Gwebinkundla, Mpisekhaya, Zwelidumile . . ."

He mouthed the syllables awkwardly, the royal genealogy moving into his tongue, flowing towards his heart as a thin linguistic branch. The incantation was something unfamiliar, but solid enough to imagine relationships of knowing, of respect, for the land in which he lived. He closed his eyes to hold onto the sounds, to place himself inside the essential ancestries, to remember. Two minutes later, however, those words – names – had disappeared from his mind. In a panic, he flipped back onto the page where he'd found them, re-recited the list, got up and wrote each one down carefully on a small card which he affixed to the wall above his desk.

He pushed his glasses from his face in frustration and pressed a small yellow buzzer on the desk. "Mrs Nair? You can send them in now," he said.

A few seconds later, his office door clicked open and three people barrelled inside, two chattering to one another, the third striding forward with his arm outstretched.

"Hey! Jacob Goldman? Man, it's a pleasure to meet you – finally, hey?" The handshake was doubled, a kind of clasp followed by a brisk pumping. "Martin Locke. And this is Tayisha, and Marla. They're the brains." A snort-laugh, and the visitor plopped himself down hard into a chair in front of Jacob's desk.

Jacob pulled himself together, effected greetings, and manoeuvred Martin Locke out of the chair he had chosen into another – one of four carefully arranged around a small glass table. "Much more appropriate," Mrs Nair had explained. "Americans like the informal-formal, not the formal-formal; you must make like it's in your lounge, you know, high-powered, low-key. I learnt it on that course."

There was a great deal of tourism talk to start with. The woman called Tayisha, tall and airbrushed-smart, gurgled at length about the glamour of the Waterfront, the spirituality of the mountain and the surprising warmth of the indigenous dwellers. "I expected it to be beautiful, you know, but I guess I was still hung up on the apartheid images, the dogs and the police vans, you know, and I didn't see how it could all work now, but hey," her mouth smiled like a puppy's, "this is awesome, it really works."

Jacob bit back his irritation, but the other woman noticed the small muscle pulsing in his jaw, put her hand lightly on Tayisha's arm and said, "Well, you know, maybe the dogs and the vans are still, like, there, in a way, too; it's tough to get past the veneers."

The way she pronounced "veneer" sprung Jacob's head into bilingual alphadrown: *ver/near*. He distinctly heard a telephone ring, although he knew (because his own office phone sported a bright orange glow when it required his attention) no such thing was audible to anyone else.

He cleared his throat, suggested that they move onto business.

The current conversation (veneers, dogs, travel) was rooted in a phone call, nine months earlier, from an American television company. A proposal for collaboration between the Cape Town-based media outfit and the American giant had gradually unfurled – slowly at first, and then with astonishing speed. Jacob had been involved from the start, initially with some reluctance (his director suspected him of anarchic tendencies and, perhaps, some anti-American sentiment), but later as an integral member of the project team. Jacob was known as one of the best location managers in the country; he had an eye that illuminated the potential of things for the camera – he could imagine the way a skyline could speak to a screenplay, he knew just which kitchen table would serve as ballast for a character's loyalty, just where the dead silver tree should be placed to suggest loneliness. His insistence that place mattered more than any actor (and should therefore be allocated more of the budget) drove his colleagues wild with irritation, but there was no debate about his competence. The man could see things.

The name of the American project was *Extreme Motherhood*. It was the second in a series. For the first, *Extreme Friendship*, network viewers had been invited to submit stories, videos, e-mails and images about the most challenging friendships they were, or had been, involved with.

From the tens of thousands of responses, some twenty or so had been selected, and for each, an hour-long programme had been created, following – Oprah-like – the tale of the friendship – dwelling on the "extremities" involved, and at the end subjecting the friends concerned to a jury, a panel of celebrity psychologists, entertainers and popular speakers. At the end of the series, the participants voted the "most extreme" by the jury had won prizes – money, cruise-ship adventures, furniture.

Extreme Friendship had been hugely successful. The first episode aired had covered the relationship between two women, Lucia and Marilyn. Lucia was tall, with blonde hair and dimples; Marilyn, in contrast, was plump, and bounced when she walked. Lucia's husband had embarked on an affair with Marilyn, and abandoned his marriage, leaving dust, debt and disaster in his wake. Lucia, determined to sabotage

35

his new life, had driven her car through his store-front window, sent Marilyn bags of dog turds through the mail, and stalked her like a dreadful mime, mimicking her gait and gestures as she tried to go about her life.

Then, one day, Marilyn met Lucia skulking outside her kitchen door, holding a large black bag. When she asked what on earth she was doing, Lucia opened the bag with a flourish, shook it hard, and yelled: "Present! You bitch!"

A fat, sleek curl dropped out onto the step – a yard of glossy snake.

Which did not move.

Marilyn had screamed. But the poor snake, dazed and no doubt unhungry, just lay there, like a coiled bundle of brown Play-Doh. Something – Lucia's wild gyrating? The snake's somnolence? – flipped in Marilyn. She began to laugh, and she had laughed so hard that she had flopped onto the grass (not far from the snake), clutching her abdomen, saying, "Ow! Ow! Oh, my God!"

Lucia had been unable to resist. She, too, had begun to giggle, and from that day on, as though the appalling squabbles had been no more than a flap in the sandpit, Marilyn and Lucia had become inseparable. The husband had been more than puzzled, but in the end resigned himself to the facts: Lucia and Marilyn had an extreme friendship, conceived in antipathy, delivered through the fantastic and now solid as frozen ice cream.

Viewing audiences adored Lucia and Marilyn; they relished the sordid stalking, the vengeful dog turds and the final collapse of hostility. The psychologists pontificated about reaction formation and sibling jealousy, and audience members raved with admiration for Lucia's publicly bad behaviour and the way the tables had been turned on the hapless husband.

Subsequent episodes pushed at the definitions both of "extreme" and of "friendship". In one story, the friendship had involved one man's rescue of another during a mountain-climbing expedition. In another, it was a child with cerebral palsy and a black-and-white dog. Most of the time, though, the nearer the episodes were to Hallmark notions of friendship, the more popular they were.

As the series aired, it was clear that a follow-up series would be essential. An audience had been created.

Several proposals circulated (all attached to egos, budgets, connections and status), and for a while it was unclear whether a second season of *Extreme Friendship* would be undertaken or whether *Extreme Something Else* would get the nod. The ins and outs of the battles were never revealed to the Cape Town company, who had been – in fact – rather oblivious to the whole "Extreme" thing until it was proposed that they become involved in the next project: *Extreme Motherhood*.

Extreme Friendship had been explicitly uninterested in two kinds of relationship: familial and romantic. *Extreme Motherhood* was different – it intended to capitalise on the fact that *Extreme Friendship* had, in the US, generated a lot more interest from women than it had from men, and to pave the way for the third series, to be entitled *Extreme Romance*. *Extreme Motherhood* was also going global, which for the American company meant including stories based in England, "somewhere in Europe" and "elsewhere", among the US scenarios.

Elsewhere turned out to mean South Africa.

"They tried a couple of other options," Jacob's director had told him at the outset of the collaboration. "Apparently, there was talk of a refugee-type story – woman walking with toddlers, attacks, camps – but the access was going to be really tough, and they decided it was too hectic. You can imagine the politics, the things you'd have to avoid, and translation always puts a barrier between the audience and the story." He paused to draw breath. "I know you don't agree, Jacob," he continued, "but this is an amazing opportunity for us – the money is great and we'll be working with XTV. We have to produce two episodes; they choose one. I want your full, and I mean full, co-operation. This is the way things are moving, and we're getting in on the ground floor."

Then, Jacob had just raised his eyebrows. "So," he replied. "South African motherhood. No refugees. No translation. And no politics."

"Shit, man!" The director slammed his palm onto the arm of the chair. "Why do you always have to be like this? I'm getting a team together. You're on it. *Extreme Motherhood – South Africa*. Must be what your bloody mother feels every time she looks at you and your cynical donkey face."

Now, eleven months later, the US team members responsible for the final selection were sitting in Jacob's office, smoothing down the fact that they owned the deal, making like friends. It would, of course, have been possible to have simply sent the completed episodes, for scrutiny and judgement, to San Francisco. But no, said the project directors, that's not how we work, this is an alliance, we've been working so closely with you, we'll send three of our guys over, and you can screen it for us, take us through things, work with us on the decision.

It was hardly as if the San Francisco people were coming to watch material new to them. From the very beginning of the contract, practically every sentence produced by the Cape Town team had been subjected to discussion, commentary, veto. Dozens of concepts had been submitted northwards for consideration, treatments had been developed, scrutinised, rejected, reworked, and when the filming had begun, several technicians and advisors from San Francisco had accompanied Jacob and the other team members everywhere. Jacob had found it exhausting, he felt like a hamster in a cage, but he had been unable to prevent himself from becoming – secretly – fascinated by the ideas, by the meaning of extreme motherhood, by the meaning of motherhood per se.

"So . . ." He opened his arms wide, and tried to smile as though he meant it. "Shall we go? I'm pretty sure it's all cued up."

"Oh, man," said Tayisha, "I just can't wait for this. I've been excited since we left. I just want to see what it looks like here," she circled her head around the room.

Jacob ushered the visiting trio through the office corridors. The screening room was already full. Jacob's director grinned at him, avuncular and completely artificial. "Ah-ha! There you are. Thought you might have taken our guests off to the beach, Jacob," he boomed, and fussily patted the seats next to him. "Sit, sit! This is it." He turned around, snapping his fingers at the technician behind him. "Let's go. You know a lot of the background, so we'll talk afterwards." He snapped his fingers again and the room darkened.

Jacob knew what was coming so intimately he could have closed his eyes and the screen images would still have flowed perfectly in front of him.

* * *

The first *Extreme Motherhood – South Africa* episode involved the story of an Afrikaans family – mother, father, daughter, large, settled in a tiny South African town – who had started, five years earlier, to offer their home to children whose parents had died of Aids. When the filming had started, seven orphaned children had been living with the family, and the episode focused on the day an eleven-year-old had appeared at the family's gate, carrying a baby – her five-month-old brother.

In the actual narrative, the battle between the Afrikaans mother and the eleven-year-old had been titanic. The older woman had wanted to take the baby, wash him, redress him, get the doctor to examine him. The child-mother had refused to let her touch him, explaining over and over in Sesotho that she was afraid he would be stolen, that they just needed some food.

Over time the fear had diminished, and the two of them, eleven-year-old and baby, had remained with the family, but there was still a hint of terror in the child's eyes as she watched the large, loud woman swabbing her tiny brother with a flannel, singing in robust terms about God and goodness.

The treatment of the story glossed over the tension, showing the two mothers managing together; the child sleeping with her arm around the baby, the woman stroking the child's head, straightening her doek.

Jacob had been uncomfortable throughout the development of the episode. His own work had been limited to the arrangement of scenes – angles within the rooms of the too-small house, choosing which children to focus on, trying to develop a visual sense of the small, dry town and its closed citizens: heads turned from the cameras in the one main street, plastic bags caught against the barbed-wire fence outside a police station, dented cars. His discomfort eddied around the sentimentalities: the overt spaciousness of the Afrikaans family's heart, the mute appreciation of the orphaned kids.

When he voiced his thoughts to Parusha, one of his team-mates, she snapped at him, "You are *so* negative, Jacob. This family *is* generous. Those children *are* happy, happi*er* than when they were sitting in some shack with a dead body. What is your problem? What would you like us to tell a story about? The Treatment Action Campaign? The Minister of Health and there-is-no-Aids-from-HIV? This is a show about motherhood. And right here are some dynamite mothers. Get over it."

Jacob felt chastened, and during the filming of the next episode, he had concentrated on his job, and tried not to think aloud.

The second story was about a woman called Khanyisile Makabela, who lived in Khayelitsha. She had opened a bed-and-breakfast in her shack, and with a canny business sense and biting sense of humour had weathered numerous start-up challenges only to find herself in the pages of the South African Airways magazine, advertising adventures in tourism. From that point on, she had roared into popularity with the ecotourism companies, and, because she described herself as mother to all those who stayed with her, became a perfect subject for *Extreme Motherhood – South Africa*.

Jacob's team followed her as she took Germans, Canadians, US visitors through the Khayelitsha streets, introducing them to neighbours, explaining how the taxi routes worked and didn't, ignoring their anxiety at the sight of chickens' heads and feet in buckets waiting to become meals. In return, the visitors, sitting at night inside the beautifully decorated shack rooms, poured out their hearts to Mama Khanyi – talking about their too-much money, their sons on drugs, their trust in Africa, their gratitude at the discovery that African people would smile at them.

The episode included footage of Khanyisile with her own mother, who lived in a tiny village high up on the east coast – the two of them attending a funeral, and the old woman waving her arm like a flag as her daughter drove away, back to Cape Town, over the long grey highway.

The final shot of Khanyisile had her with her arms around a blond child. She was saying, "This boy, too, he lives in America, but I am his mother also, I am his mother because I am teaching him about the way people must be with one another, and learn about one another, that is a mother's job, she is there to teach the world, and that is the way we will have peace."

The shot faded with the boy tilting his chin up towards her, leaning his body into her stomach.

Jacob didn't know which episode worried him most. His own version of extreme motherhood had no saints in it. Extreme motherhood for Jacob meant a soaking wet pillow and a sense of impotence so drastic he had lost his breath.

* * *

Jacob's motherhood had begun the day his wife had put an end to hers. For four weeks, the two of them had struggled.

"It's the wrong time, Jacob," she'd said, "I just don't . . ."

"What?" he answered, tight with anxiety. "You don't what?"

For as long as he could remember, Jacob had been interested in children. He had grown up without brothers and sisters, a surprise to his parents who were both in their early forties when he was born. They had been affectionate, but distant – slightly awkward with his energy and curiosity, happiest when he was in his room, absorbed by a project, feeding a bird dropped from the nest, drawing a picture of tadpoles.

From early on, he had migrated emotionally into the families of his school friends, the larger the family the better. His favourite family included six children (two the offspring of a sister-in-law who lived somewhere else), and a grandmother who seemed to sit permanently at the kitchen table, drinking dark tea and delivering opinions on character, weather, washing. He longed for the day he would have his own family, the surge and noise of voices, the thud of feet scampering, the impossible balance of loving this one and that one, too, always.

When he and Sarah had married, she had agreed that babies were a good idea, but warned that she was not "the mothering type". He had been so in love with her – the way she made darkly sardonic jokes, the fact that she was afraid of jellyfish, her shoulder blades in the dark – that he hadn't paid attention to her caution about children, believing that the love, the home, the life they'd share would inevitably (almost without their having anything to do with it) create sons, daughters.

After five years, however, her lack of interest in pregnancy hadn't changed and now, here they sat, across from one another in the blue-and-white living room.

"What? You don't what?"

"Jacob. It's not that easy. I don't . . . It's not about you. Or us. But I don't really want a baby. I don't think I want children."

Jacob looked at her. "You don't now?"

"No. It's not now."

He misunderstood. "But if not now, when? What's your plan?"

"No. It's not 'I don't want a baby now'. It's 'I don't want a baby ever'. I don't want to be a mother." As Jacob said nothing, she rushed on. "It's been so long I've been thinking this, Jacob. And I knew . . ." she faltered. "I knew you wanted something different. So, I didn't speak, I didn't say anything. When it happened, I didn't even want to tell you."

"You didn't want to tell me?"

The morning Sarah had, with a shy kind of wriggle, told him that she thought they'd slipped up, she thought she was pregnant, he had been beside himself with delight. He had whooped, and shouted, and run around the small garden like a madman. The neighbour's cat had sprung up onto the wall behind him, tail bushed like a peacock's, as he did a handspring on the lawn, falling onto his stomach with a thump and howling with laughter.

Sarah, watching him, said, "You're a nut in a nut jar, darling . . ." and had left for work almost immediately.

He had pulled himself together, but spent hours of the rest of the day staring out of the window into the sunlight in a trance. Everything was beginning. Everything was going to be right.

But then it had become clear from Sarah's silences, her strange word-lessness, that not everything was right. They had spoken, at first tentatively, then with increasing terror. Now, she repeated: "I didn't want to tell you."

Jacob got up and walked towards the bookcase. He ran his fingers slowly over the spines of the books. "But you did tell me, Sarah," he said. "I want this baby. I think I've been waiting for this baby all my life. What are we going to do?"

Sarah flinched. She didn't begin to cry, but her breath caught in her throat like a cough. The words she said were impossible. "Jacob. The baby's gone."

* * *

He had lain on his bed. The counterpane smelled of vanilla, the tears dripped and dripped out of his eyes, the pillowcase damp and damper as the hours crawled by, his body becoming cavernous.

He could not – in his head – put Sarah's body on any kind of doctor's table, choose an instrument, look at the bloody matter, position Sarah's abdomen in cramping pain. He could not manage the location.

There isn't a baby any more.

The unimaginable pictures swam around the room, ghost shapes, threatening to swallow him: the sound of tiny feet, a laugh, Sarah talking to a nurse, a conspiracy.

The phone rang in another room. He could hear Sarah's tone, full of anxiety, murmuring, but he couldn't hear the words.

Jacob's discernment – motherhood as loss, as yearning beyond understanding – had made his work a torture. He hadn't even tried to address the chasm between himself and Sarah; it took him all his strength to find a connection to his own clothes, his front door key, syntax. The *Extreme Motherhood – South Africa* episodes felt like lies, plump with the benign care of women, reaching all over the world under beaming approval.

* * *

The tape in the screening room whirred, and the lights came back up as hands clapped wildly and voices murmured in approval, rubbing against one another.

Jacob realised he could not stay. Abruptly, he pushed himself out of his seat and headed for the door, ignoring the shouts – "Jacob? Jacob?" – behind him. Mute with grief, he plunged into the street, crashing into passers-by, head down, breathing too hard. *I have lost my child*, he thought, *I will never recover.*

If Jacob had not been striding blindly, fighting for balance, he might have felt their breath – the breath of the royal genealogy around him – thick with sweetness, claiming alliance with him. If, in his loneliness, he could have listened, he would have heard the ancestral grandmothers explain that, with a little patience – and holding the sharp end of the knife – revolutions come, children will be born. In the history of the land, they said (still rubbing tears from their cheeks), children could get taken away. Stolen. It was not the end of the story.

But Jacob was not yet ready. His sobs were cracking his ribs. His heart leaking wet patches soft on his shirt.

Thought control

No sooner had one thought arisen in her mind, than another, swimming in completely the opposite direction, came into view. It actually felt like the first move of an elementary computer programme, or a problem in basic logic: *if x, then y* (as opposed to: *if x, then more of x*).

Perhaps it was the residue of her father's unremitting attempts to get her to understand the rudiments of chess. Still, at eighty-four, he managed to beat the electronic Chessmaster he had been given by one of her sisters. He struggled to remember how to turn the damn thing on, but could checkmate it in twenty moves. His efforts to train her into an adequate chess player had included the design of large chessboards in the garden, where huge wooden kings and queens towered over her head, and the furious-looking flat-faced knight had to be lugged awkwardly over patches of light and dark gravel: "Carefully, J! Your shoes are scuffing up the squares. Lift it, don't drag . . ."

She was a hopeless chess player, but perhaps something had, after all, sunk in.

Her current problem was one of ethics. She wanted to cast a spell. And the very act of spell-casting entails the readiness to exert will, to control the planet, to have things her own way. So that was wrong.

But, what was also wrong was passivity.

Sitting there, doing nothing, letting oneself fall into abjection and the realm of the squashed. No. That was indisputably wrong, too. Action was essential; and one kind of action entailed careful prayer, meditation, holding out to the universe for the best outcome for all sentient beings. Another of course suggested that the focus on sentient beings all over the place was a form of cowardice: she needed to claim her desire. Which would never be realised without her fulsome and passionate co-operation. The secret was to imagine one's heart's desire with such commitment and clarity that the atomic energies of the galaxy simply parted, and the treasure swam cleanly into one's arms.

The reason she needed a spell was simple. She wanted to talk to someone and the someone did not want to talk to her. In such a situation, options are limited. You can gracefully accept, go gently into that good night; you can rage, rage against the dying, but you can't rage forever, your throat gets sore. And when you are quiet again, it's not as though anything has changed. She's still not talking to you.

You have to cope with the rock truth of the matter: the someone is sealed behind a no contact vow; sailing, sailed and gone.

Spell-casting is an ancient art. It is not a matter of cloaks and wands, said the books. Spell-casting does, indeed, demand technologies but much more importantly, it demands dispassion, a certain relation to disembodiedness, a recognition of how small we are in comparison to how overwhelmingly complex, multi-hued and mercurial the energies around us. Mastery of humility is the key; the spellcaster's heart needs to be a perfect crimson null, ready to pour its beating into calligraphies of force he will never understand or own, no matter how majestic the paraphernalia of colours, potions, smoke, fire. This is what she read.

It sounded very difficult, and she wondered how it all sat together – the meditators on their cushions with the sentient beings, the sangomas and their supplicants, blowing breath three times into the bones for access to the ancestors, the train of little red-and-white boys psalming up a cathedral aisle, and the spellcasters with their crimson, zero-shaped hearts. Syncretism a sin, according to Roman orthodoxy – and where on earth did they fit? Spellcasters, for sure . . . in Mexico City, she had seen a woman in a soaring colonial cathedral carefully locking a brass key into a huge mound of padlocks, other keys, ribbons, in front of a glass case housing the remains of a saint, the relics visible as thinly grey, cracked, branches of bone. A notice explained, in Spanish, that the saint would ensure that the mouths of those who knew your secret were locked for ever.

She was not, however, in a position to fret about philosophical incontinence or incoherence. While it was clear that substantial squabbles differentiated approaches to assistance, everyone seemed to agree that in an emergency (such as being born or having a wild-tongued neighbour), help could be found. She turned to her principal source of wisdom in all challenges of the soul: the internet.

The Berkeley Magick Astrological Foundation was one of a number of seemingly prestigious organisations offering a vast array of magical devices to internet users far and wide. For the price of a credit card number, mailed to you could be a Wanga Doll, an Obeah Spell, an Extreme Retrieve a Lover Incantation, an Exact Revenge Amulet, or a specially personalised bracelet from Aurora, the White Witch of Light. The website had a page full of testimony from grateful customers: *I was down to my last dollar and didn't know what was going to happen. I asked Aurora for help and a week later, I won $435 at tenpin bowling, thank you so much, I knew you would come through for me, Aurora.*

It looked perfect. She scrutinised the dolls and the amulets, but their images didn't look so convincing. The dolls reminded her of the small beaded ones, sold to tourists by collectives of women, who attached scarlet ribbons to the dolls' necks and labels that said: *Siyabonga! Thank you! You have helped a child with HIV.*

An Extreme Incantation seemed a bit greedy. It was true that she wanted the someone around, but Extreme Incantation implied earthquakes, tsunamis of transformation, and maybe she would turn to that later, but not now.

In the end, she chose the Restore Harmony Spell. Into the little box on her screen, she typed the someone's name, and explained (although she was not prompted to do this) that she loved the someone and would look after her very carefully, she promised, this time. That she had been, before, precipitous, taken risks with precious things; she would do better. Her credit card number was demanded, and the screen informed her that further instructions and a date for the spell setting would be sent to her in the mail.

As she looked at the box that blinked "Send Now", she felt a little queasy. The logistics struck her as full of loopholes – how would the spell-casters know where to find the someone all the way from Berkeley? Wasn't it wrong, anyway, to be trying to cast spells? Surely the someone, with a mind of her own, should be left to make her own decisions? And both of them had such common names – what if the spell mixed up her someone with the millions of other someones out there? It was a scary thought.

* * *

Six years earlier, it had been she herself who had been the target of a spell. It had all begun with a phone call.

"Thank goodness it's you," said her friend, who had been a long way away. "It's crazy here. I can't talk to anyone. How on earth did you get through?"

It hadn't been until days later that she realised how miraculous it actually was; newspapers and magazines were replete with stories of relatives from all over the globe punching desperately at the numbers: "212, 914, 718 . . . Where are you? Pick up, pick up . . ."

She had got through from seventeen thousand miles away on the first try, and there was her friend, a slight time delay punctuating her sentences oddly, but sounding both robust and mightily pissed off.

"It's appalling. I feel as though someone is going to come in and shoot me if I say one word of what I'm thinking – the doorman, the next-door neighbour with his kid, even Sandra, for that matter."

They'd met, seven years earlier through a personals advertisement. The story of the advert was convoluted. Another friend, irritated by her habit of cleaving irresponsibly and clam-like to women who barely gave her the time of day, placed an ad on her behalf in a popular city newspaper. The ad read: *GF, 30, into ideas and politics, but lazy, small, minimal hair, seeks GF interested in words, sex and the city, any race okay, over 40 a plus.*

She had been amused, although a little embarrassed by the *lazy* and the *sex*, but had read all the replies posted to her mailbox. One explained that it was looking for someone to party with, and that it had to be frank, recreational drugs were cool. Another wrote three pages about the death of its previous lover and spoke of needing to "embrace again life's joyous possibilities". A typed one, from a lesbian (as opposed to any kind of GF), talked of an interest in socialism, a passionate anti-Zionism and a Jewish identity and listed the last four books she had read. J had been immediately intrigued and had made arrangements to meet the socialist, literate surveyor of the personals. Whose name turned out to be Red.

Red was an extraordinary woman, who sometimes dressed as a man, spoke with an enchanting British lisp and whose generosity over the years they were friends in the same city defied description: trips to islands lapped by translucent sea, caretaking through an awkward and frightening illness, patience with suspected infidelities. Red's politics throughout their relationship were simultaneously scarlet and purple – both in unrepentant shades. Purple was for the queer – marching through the city streets yelling about the way the government murdered HIV-positive young men in their thousands, doling out clean needles to Lower East Side junkies with skeletal bodies and mischievous eyes as part of political activism. Scarlet was for the antimilitarism, the rage against the tanks spew-wading onto Islamic sands, the cheques sent to organisations pledging help to desperate immigrants.

So she could guess at Red's opinions concerning towers, planes, and the innocence of lives lost.

"Where was Sandra? Is she okay?"

Sandra was her friend's lover, a sweet-faced woman who knew more about butch and femme than anything the queer encyclopedia had yet put together. J didn't know her well, but it was clear the relationship was full of vibrancy – idiosyncratic and alive. Her friend – at sixty-three – took tango lessons with Sandra, went rocketing across snow deserts in sleds pulled by husky teams, wrote books about early twentieth-century lesbian communists, which she dedicated to her own lovers, and it was clear Sandra was a match for, even a spur to, such adventure.

"Sandra was at work. Her office is fifteen blocks from those towers, she saw everything, and she's freaked as a freak out. She could see people jumping. By the time she made it home – she walked, all eighty-whatever blocks, through ash like sludge – she was beside herself and I was the one flying the plane, flying both planes. All she could say was that she was sure I was glad it had happened."

* * *

J had spent the rest of the evening at home, squatting on a bed, stuck to the images of plane-attack which ran, over and over and over, through a series of talking CNN heads who were as lost for new words as she'd ever seen them. Planes pierced like tiny silver fish knives, buildings crumble-dissolved downwards, black debris rained from the sun, people ran and ran, faces twisted over their shoulders. The same planes, the same collapsings, ticker-tape information, other planes, other buildings, cellphone calls, scrolling on and on beneath the mouthing heads. She thought of the eyes of the pilots, a plane-nose away from the sheer vertical of windows. Were they praying? Was there a microsecond where someone caught someone else's eye through the panes, mouths aghast-open? Did anyone vow: "This is for them, this is for my children . . ."?

Did someone raise a fist?

"Amandla! Ngawethu!"

Long before the planes had glided into the Towers, fists had been raised. Not so far from the Towers, and in many US cities. She herself had raised one. Direct United States investment in South Africa in the year 1960 was estimated at about two hundred million dollars; by 1982, it was two thousand, six hundred and fifty million dollars and rising. The steepest growth curve of the investment took place between 1973 and 1980 – on the graphs of the analysts it was practically a straight upward line. The last (but who knew, then, that they were the last?) decades of apartheid policies were partnered by the phrase "constructive engagement". The "engagement" was odd because the marriage was already well in its groove; the "constructive" was about vocabulary: "violent" meant black people with weapons, stones, guns, rights, any kind of a weapon, "constructive" meant "not violent".

She had witnessed hunger strikes of protest, held in the last months of city winter in front of blockaded buildings, people sleeping in makeshift tents and thick cocoons of blankets, talking in huddled groups about the theft of land.

In her own cocoon, she drew people maps of South Africa, with eighty-one little squiggles showing Bantustans. Sometimes she was sceptical. Speeches about the sameness of Biko and Mandela bugged her. Black South Africans got adopted as sudden, exotic heroes and heroines, and then what? Dropped, abandoned, as their visas became a problem for civil disobedience. Psychotic men haunted the fringes, muttering about Vietnam, war machines, begging for extra cups of coffee. Strange political splits emerged – this lot not radical enough, that lot secretly racist, this one really an apartheid spy, that one sexing with the wrong girl or boy.

One morning, she had dragged herself towards a shower, towards the wait for a shower, and wondered whether or not to spend money on breakfast. Suddenly, there was a roar, a shouting so deep the railings around the grass seemed to reverberate. She turned her head to see a tidal wave of banners pouring through the wrought-iron gates of the university, rows and rows of mostly black men and women marching, striding, down the boulevard. There must have been five thousand, singing, chanting. Someone standing next to her breathed: "It's Harlem! Harlem is marching on the university. Their worst nightmare. A-fucking-mazing, man!"

When first-years enrolled at the university, they were all given a map of the city, with explicit instructions not to go above 125th Street, unless they knew the area well already. The western streets bordering the campus were "okay", the eastern ones not: "You don't wanna go there on your own – drug scenes, crazy people."

That Saturday morning had rolled everyone together in a tight ball: blue-and-brown suited New York riot cops in big white vans screamed onto the campus, dozens of them rocketing onto the mushy lawns and parking halfway up the steps. Tear gas was fired at the gates, causing banners to be ripped into scarves to protect faces and eyes; people ran frantically from one university gate to another, only to be greeted by helmets, batons, snarling Alsatians on throat-tight leashes. Bricks were hurled into classroom windows, garbage cans used as shields, thick police thighs waded through the people huddled in front of the blockaded building, tearing away posters and flimsy tent decorations, yelling, sweeping batons in front of them like scythes.

She had found herself, bunched together with dozens of others, in a pen marked out by yellow police tape, strung between trees: "You're under arrest! You are all under arrest! Do not try to run, do not commit disorder. You are trespassing. You are under arrest."

It had been nearly the next day before she was back on the streets, spat out of the system, a "student protestor". They'd been cramped into small, green, wire-mesh cages downtown; no toilets, no phone calls. She had been slightly worried, but not too much, given how many of them there were, given what prisons looked like in other configurations she knew of. But many around her were gaunt with shock, shaking, enraged or tearful: "They aren't allowed to do that, the police only get to come with the permission of the university, I can't believe this, they gave them permission! They let them come and get us!"

One lanky co-inmate had been irritated by the laments: "Man, grow up. They came because of the union guys marching in. No one cares about us. One row of black guys and you're toast, man. You saw it."

A woman had asked for help with changing a tampon: "Please make a circle around me, just let me do it without them looking."

She herself was very thirsty. She had propped herself up against the mesh until a baton poked through at her: "You, get away from the edge. Commie bitch."

She stared at the speaker – little eyes, moustache, a dribble of yellow on his collar.

"Not so clever, hey?" he hissed. "Your little Africa friends get you in trouble? Oooh, baby. So sorry, baby."

She had not, however, piloted any planes. She had returned to South Africa, grown her hair, found a job and a lover and even as taxis got branded with the name Tupac, as her children yearned for McDonald's, as Esiquithini – the Island – was hawked, she had taken no flying lessons.

Worse than that.

Four years after the call to Red, she visited the city again. It was a whirlwind trip, three days only, carved from between obligations. It had been February, the wind bitter, patches of ice on the pavements. Her borrowed boots skidded, her heart raced to be back in the streets she loved like a mantra. She stayed with Red and Sandra, and packed herself into the crowd of thousands protesting the then possibility of US war against Iraq. Someone gave her a poster to hold: *They found a dangerous warhead in the White House* – a picture of Bush's head on its side, looking like a lopped lettuce.

And then she had taken the subway to the site of the Twin Towers.

It had been surrounded by high silver wire mesh: a large square, flat grey floor, surrounded by a careful series of enlarged photographs, museum-like. Across the road, tucked into more wire mesh, was a battered paper-and-cloth collage of notes, dedications, poems, messages, bits of clothing, caps. *We will never forget*. Small tables with dozens of tiny glass Twin Tower replicas, all whole.

A group of Korean tourists descended from a bus, as she stood staring at the gap. What they must have thought, heaven only knows – with a rainbow afghan scarf wrapped around her neck, she had cried like a banshee.

There had been such a hole in the sky.

On the subway back, there had been a child's poem among the advertisements for health insurance and headache pills: *From my window/I could see/The tallest buildings/I ever did see/Now they are gone/And my window has nowhere to go.*

She had felt bewitched, sucked into a vacuum of perspective, wiped out by being ordinary, unable to fly a plane, unable to bear the plane's flight, she couldn't even get off the subway.

* * *

"Hey!" A voice startled her. "What are you still doing here?"

J jumped, back across six years, a soft guilt edging at her throat. Her computer screen was glowing. The pink box – "Send Now" – blinked.

The spell was still waiting for transmission.

"I'm about to leave," said the voice. "If I have to write one more word about structural adjustment programmes, I will just about explode. Come and have a drink with me. You look like you need a whisky."

J turned and smiled at her colleague in the doorway, a glass-elegant woman too smart for her own good and twice as funny.

J swivelled back to the computer, stared hard at the invitation of magic and switched the whole thing off with a clean, strange little shudder.

No spell.

She would ask for no spell.

* * *

Across the city, the someone sat quietly on an amber couch, reading a book about beekeeping, with a glass of white wine on the table in front of her. She was feeling peaceful. Her day had been demanding: cantankerous colleagues, heart-wrenching requests, multitasking so dense she'd felt like a diasporic tribe instead of a single human being. Hearing the phone ring in her neighbour's flat, she was glad it wasn't for her. Her heart settled, slowly calm, and into the city dusk as she lit candles against the night, she sent up a small prayer:

"Thank you."

Disarmament

Her stars said: *This is a period in which you will find yourself knowing what other people are feeling. While it isn't unusual for you, as a fish, to be sensitive to the waters around you, you may be feeling that you know more than you want to. Remember that others' anxieties, angers and desires probably have very little to do with you. You can see them. This doesn't mean they can see you.*

To her, that didn't seem right at all. It was the other way round. All too visible is what she felt. And as for *them*, where were they?

The morning headline stamped out, in letters five centimetres high, the rape of a baby. Although the words had blocked themselves into her eyes as soon as she'd bought the pages, she read the whole paper – including her horoscope – before entering negotiations.

The train was full; her bag squashed into her lap like an awkward puppy, her legs tucked away against the sharp knees of the man opposite whose thumbs tap-danced on a cellphone. She was wearing a new, bright orange top, but had noticed as she'd sat waiting for the train that morning, that with the flaming T-shirt, bright blue rucksack and pale face, she reminded herself of the old national flag.

The opening gambit involved duty. It was her duty to read about the baby's rape. The baby would be less raped if she knew a story about her, a story with some details – age (not weight), where, how did they know, where was mom. Counter-argument said that, no, if she became a reader, a reader in the aftermath of the baby's rape, she would be part of the attack, her eyes boring into the tiny squalling body. Disgustedly in response came the voice of the activist: information is power, a paragraph of information is not a baby, it signposts a site of war, it alerts the strategist. Futile, wailed the smallest voice, futile.

After she'd read the paragraphs, deconstructive tools leaped forward to sever linguistic skeins, expose hierarchies and interests, but it was too late. Tears streaked down her face, and by the time the train stopped at her station, the cellphone man was patting her arm and twelve other passengers were carefully ignoring her, holding themselves like closed umbrellas politely away from her body.

She stepped awkwardly onto the platform, gave the sea air a hopeful sniff, wiped her nose on the shoulder of an orange sleeve and realised things could not continue.

* * *

"They have to be turned in," said her friend firmly. "It's enough. It's been enough for a long time. There will be repercussions and costs, and we'll need to figure out how to handle those who just refuse, or attempt to hide them. But if motor companies can recall faulty vehicles, even really expensive ones, we can do this."

"Where shall we put them?" she asked. "They're not that big, but we're talking millions."

"Plant them? This is a gigantic country, lots of soil, sand, gravel, river bed, grassland. It'll mean extensive, and I mean extensive, planning, but if the IEC can get us all onto a voters' roll, I don't see why imagination and will can't get this organised."

She wriggled her eyebrows, anxiously. "But how will it work? They get turned in, and planted right away? They get stored, and transported to planting zones? And what if people want to plant their own? Just for remembrance, or for political reasons."

He snorted. "Nobody will want to plant their own. Unless the fools want to go dig it up again, try resuscitation or some such idiocy. No one is willingly going to see his get put into the ground."

She thought for a bit. "People are going to apply for exemptions, you know. Claim self-defence, or ask for a special permit. Or they'll hand in one, and try and get another illegally elsewhere. We'll face a whole black market thing."

His face darkened with rage, so brown his skin looked purple under his cheekbones. "No one will be granted an exemption. No one can claim a special permit. That rape, it was the last one."

She winced inwardly, a little, but her friend was beside himself with fury, and he was the president. A little rhetoric seemed justifiable.

* * *

The next few days were indescribable. The proclamation part was simple enough: computer-generated SMSs streamed in their millions into cellphones. Teletype messaging invaded all news broadcasts, sitcoms, *Idols* episodes and game shows. All radio stations spoke of the presidential decree – in seventeen languages (Portuguese, French, Kiswahili, Arabic, and several versions of cool urban Mzansi-thetha were absorbed into the official language list). Newspapers trumpeted times, places, procedures. Finally, priests, imams, doctors, sangomas, primary school principals and rugby coaches received personal visits to ensure that they knew how to spread the word: "Those things have to be handed in. It's over. No exceptions. No bargains. No questions."

What happened following the proclamation, however, defied prediction. In most places, the decree was met by roars of laughter. But as the severity of the president's intention became clear, gross panic beset the nation. Some raced for the country's borders. Others stockpiled weapons and vowed to defend themselves to the death. A group of senior military officials with corporate connections attempted to assassinate the president as he ate his breakfast. Whole families committed spectacular – but obscene – suicide in public spaces. The currency's value plunged, as global voices caught wind of the decree and responded with outrage and disbelief.

The friend remained unmoved and, at exactly the hour he had proclaimed, every human penis in the country was turned in. One moment they hung – curled or stiff, tucked or loose, chilled or comfortable – between a pair of legs, the next, they were gone. It happened so fast that most owners experienced no more than a sharp microslice of pain, like a paper cut, a frustration rather than a wound.

She held her breath.

She was waiting for the women. Would their keening, the loss of the supple rods of desire they'd held and circled, reverse the proclamation? She was waiting for the men. Would they still be able to move, so out of balance with themselves, full of a hole?

She was waiting for sound. Would language dissolve into meaningless burble? Would the words and the syntax deflate, dissolve into indistinguishable sounds, "a" sound like "s", babies lose the ability to tell a consonant from a glide, lose access to differentiation?

She was waiting for God, and for the ancestors. Would the Holy Spirit cry, become stricken with a grief too strong for the trees? Would the ancestors be unable to appear, unable to demand their beer, to insist on hospitality?

She sat on the balcony of her small house, rocking to evade the bizarre cacophonies in the air around her. She wondered where her friend was, and felt slightly irritated by the persistent purr of the tortoiseshell cat on her lap. The baby knocked at her half-open door, lightly, and swam in, turtling herself neatly into a cushion on the floor.

"Wait," she said, "that cushion has catfur on it. It's not clean."

The baby smiled at her, quizzically.

She felt deeply ashamed. "Not clean. I'm sorry. I guess maybe you've been places where clean isn't –" She stopped, unable to get herself out of the mud, trying not to stare at the bandages, the trackmarks of needles, the awkward way the baby held her limbs and neck.

"Actually, the hospital people were obsessed with 'clean'," said the baby. "Don't worry, the cushion is easy for me."

She sat still, frozen with the death of the headline, paralysed with wanting the baby not to know what the baby knew, mute-slow in smallness, the fact that the penis had raped the baby and not her.

"I wanted to tell you two things." The baby spoke oddly, as though she was translating, or unsure of the way language was supposed to work.

"The one is about the decree. I'm glad your friend did that. I wish he'd done it sooner. It was so brave, and I'm amazed. He's a brave man. Please tell him for me."

She looked at the baby, clearly in pain on the cushion, and bit the insides of her lip so as not to sob.

"The other is something you know. And you know you know it, but you didn't tell your friend. And perhaps he knows, too, but neither of you could cope with me being twenty-six inches long and the penis being about five, maybe measurement got in your way. You know that the problem wasn't the penis. I mean, it was, for me, in a big way, but you know what I am saying. The problem is the head, what's in the head. It's their heads."

All the "you knows" from the baby, and the orange glow of the late afternoon sun, made her feel dizzy and wasted, spun out of the next move.

She sighed, and reached over to the baby, gently. "Would you like a blanket? It gets cold when the sun goes down here. We must contact someone to let them know you're safe."

"Safe?" The baby twisted. "I don't think so. Have you read your stars?"

Their eyes held, elongating the time between them. She shook the cat off her knees and shuffled over, on her knees, towards the cushion.

"I don't know," she said. "I'm not sure if we could have done the heads. What would have been left? Whose head would have stayed on their shoulders? Maybe even my friend would have been decapitated."

The baby's body rose up, off the cushion, a bandaged feather, spinning very slowly until her head clearly lay snug in the crook of an arm, or a wing shaft. She watched as the small figure curled fingers together, and disappeared, dissolving light and clean as a quick kiss. There was a curvy dip in the cushion's blue, still warm. She dropped her own head into the space left behind and willed it to be taken next.

Porcupine

"I hate this stuff," said the woman with the oddly soft hair, whose slipperiness caught me, always, off guard. "People want stories. They don't
want complicated 'How is the story constructed?', and 'Let's make
clever remarks about syntax' shit."

She used a whip of her blue pen to X out several pages of my most
recent writing. I didn't mind that because, firstly, she was a very interesting lover, and because, secondly, I knew she was wrong about
people and stories. I knew some people wanted to know everything
possible about stories' architecture. Some of them, like me, had ancestors whose entrails lined the drawing plans, caused the buildings
to reek of erasure. Some of them knew all about trusting the story only
to discover, years later, that its plot had lied; that the prince wanted

the princess dead not free, that the adventurers' victory had destroyed their minds, that the savages were philosophers, artists, and bankers.

The statistics have been stable for centuries; the babies of the caretakers died with much more frequency than those in the caretakers' care. It's not a riddle.

* * *

It was a Sunday afternoon and my university residence roommate was crying. I had work to do, and I wanted her to get over to her own side of the room, but her heaving worried me – her face was covered with water but something inside wasn't wet. I said, "It's okay, Serena . . ." and of course, that started it.

"It's not okay," she snapped, and blew her nose hard. "There's nothing okay about it. Whatever I think, whatever I say, it has no effect and I catch it from everyone. If I don't say anything, the racism just sits there like a blob on his lectern, and if I do say something, it's like I'm some white liberal do-gooder, and I can feel everyone around me rolling their eyes. There's nothing I can do that's right."

In her world, there is a right and a wrong thing to do about racism. That is the first chasm between us. And in her world, racism is an event, an unfortunate incident. That is the second.

We are both social science majors. We both like haloumi – and swipe snippets out of the salad bar in the dining room as often as we can. We are both scared of roaches, soggy bath towels and the undergraduate office. Because of this, she likes introducing me to her friends, and occasionally to family members who visit, by putting her arm around my shoulders – a pose – and saying, "Maki and I could be twins."

What annoys me most about this isn't the physical familiarity, or even the fact that she doesn't know me well enough to claim this kind of family acquaintance, no, what annoys me is her language.

If she didn't think "black", she wouldn't use "twin". We are not family. We are not equal. We are not the same.

She tells me that she wants to discuss things she's read about Africa – anthropology, liberation guerrillas and Catherine MacKinnon's belief that one can discuss stuff about women regardless of whether those women are called Jane or Jalisa. She brings me her ideas as though millions had not already understood the patterns of racism so deeply that they lived to a ripe old age in spite of. And, in return, I feel tethered, roped to the first rung of someone else's autobiography. I want to run and jump and soar, and never again be forced round this story, never again be so fucking bored. If I'm lucky I'll live another fifty years, and I want that life, I want every colour, accent, abyss, scent within it, but guess what, I can't say even one syllable of this to her, because, right now, she's crying at the end of my bed about the difficulty of doing the right thing, rehearsing "white woman".

And on top of everything else, I said, "It's okay, Serena . . ."

Why did you reassure her, speak to her even? Why didn't you ask for another roommate? You don't have to be nice. It's your fault. Speak up.

When I speak up in this place of higher education, this place of small rooms and heads around seminar tables, when I speak up and say, "Porcupine", I'm usually asked to repeat myself.

Heads turn and ask one another, "What did she say?", as an enormous porcupine with a mohawk of spines scurries across the floor, claws scratching the wood. Sometimes the white woman tutor sees it too, and calls it "a complex challenge". Her eyes look serious as she says this, and although I remain ignored, heads nod.

If I say, "Serena, if I have to hear once more about your wounds, how you earned them on my behalf, how I now, in the privacy of 'our' room, our domestic space, should comfort you, appreciate that you are brave, individual, innocent, I shall first eviscerate you, and then demand of your bones that they build a sewer."

But if I do this she will claim bewilderment or criticise my morality. She will, passive-aggressive, shrink away from my anger. Even worse, she may look at me with fixed blue eyes, nod and say, "I understand. You can talk to me, you know. I think you're great. I don't know what I'd do without you."

I have all these stories, all these "ifs" – always always déjà vu, lu, reçu, pu-trid. Cru-de, dude, do-ed, through, blue, tried and true-d. Familiarity does not always breed contempt – a sharp-edged, useful emotion. Familiarity can breed exhaustion, diseases of the heart.

I have other stories.

* * *

Last night, things were complicated. My white lover – the woman with the fine hair, the woman who says, "Molo, umhlobo wam" with precision to people cleaning the rubbish up off the streets because her South African Communist Party family impressed upon her the importance of camaraderie with labourers – cooked me dinner and told me she wanted to visit me in Zimbabwe. I took this statement in not exactly my stride, but a stride of relative nonchalance, because although I wouldn't have dreamed of asking her to visit me in Zimbabwe, and although I find meals with people I barely know difficult, she had, after all, looked into my vagina and said, "Okay, what do we have here?"

The trouble started when I gave her a bottle of wine – for after dinner, for some other occasion. The bottle was curly and olive green and expensive. "It's not a present," I said, when she explained to me that she didn't want me to give her "things".

At first I worried, then I let it be; then she pulled at my hair, braided and tight, very hard and when I said, in a parenthesis, I hadn't thought she was into that, she replied that tonight she felt like hitting me. I was stupid enough not to look in the mirror to find out whose eyes she was seeing.

She drew a picture on a pale napkin, circles, eyes, cone-heads, triangles. "Guess what this is?" she said. I had no idea. "I met some woman at a poetry reading in Atlanta when I went over there last year," she said. "We were talking about the American south, and she drew this to show me. Some kid in her classroom had shown it to her."

The design meant nothing to me.

"Last thing a black guy in the US sees after the Klan's thrown him down a well," she said, with absolutely no affect at all.

The lines jumped obscenely into focus for me. My stomach rose against her cooking, her sure-footed mix-and-match nonchalance, her entitled provocations. I didn't want to look at her mouth any more and demanded that she tear up the napkin. She snort-laughed at me, said, "You think that'll get rid of it? You think I'm a racist for showing it to you?"

Later, she asked me if I knew any jokes that are told against white people by black people. I know quite a lot of jokes about white idiocies on farms, about white policemen in Soweto; some I had heard on the radio, some I just knew. I said I did, and she said, "Tell me one."

She lay on her back, her seal-face inquiring as though she was asking for a marshmallow, and I said, "No."

We were two women who had liked touching each other; our skins had spoken. What would it mean to swap jokes as though we weren't on opposite sides of the land? But I didn't explain my reasoning. It was a feeling. I felt mocked and silly and cut into/against. The wine bottle caught the streetlight from outside, it glinted. "Come on," she said, "you can tell me."

I knew I would lose her hands, the attention of her thrusts and the wrap of her shoulders. I didn't know I would lose her opinions, her interest in my writing. I didn't know I would metamorphose into someone whom she said didn't see her. She told me to leave, said she didn't want to be manipulated, didn't want to feel as though I had expectations of her.

The terrible part was that I minded.

I minded what I'd seen, my mouth inside her, I minded the meaning of lovers.

I minded that, of my family – had I ever been able to tell them a word of my story (the life of a student among aliens) – none of them would have allowed me these arguments of the body. None except my youngest brother, the one my mother threatened to send to Ingutsheni, the loony bin, ten miles outside Bulawayo, the place I was, it seems so fucking long ago, born.

Contracts

It was true that Julia had drunk one too many glasses of red wine (i.e. two), and it was also true that the phone call for which she was waiting weighed far too heavily on her mind.

Sitting in a meeting surrounded by battered women, masquerading badly as activists and policy advocates, she had decided that tonight was the night she would be stripped of her cellphone, library card and keys on the train, and had made plans to avoid the loss of the most useful items in her rucksack. She had stuffed her sim card into bumblebee-embroidered socks, clipped her keys to her waistband in wannabe-macho insouciance and put on the expensive spectacles she was supposed to wear all the time, but actually drew upon only in cases of dire visual emergency (such as movie subtitles).

The scenario of the robbery was clear in her mind: there would be men, edgy and loud, dancing with demand; the shimmer of the platform lights on their coat sleeves. They would move through the train carriage, shouting and hitting the ceiling, the seats, yelling about what they were up to and what they wanted. Her rucksack would go (heavy with books about organisational development), she would hand over her bottom-of-the-range cellphone and try to extract her office keys. Would one of the men take a swing at her as he strode bluntly by, face matt with aggression? Or would she slip past their line of vision, too obedient in her handing-over for wanton attention?

But by the time the train arrived, the inevitability of the scenario had faded. The night air was sharp with salt and kelp, the platform lights hummed yellow, haloed by insects. The station wall sported a triptych of a bizarrely proportioned woman in a tangerine bikini, striding along the dock holding a fishing rod. There was no sign of a robber. What there was, however, as she walked up onto the road outside the station, was the woman in the wheelchair.

She was tiny, with a pointed face and a purple shawl. Sometimes, she had a child with her, a girl of five or six, who sat next to the wheelchair, holding tightly onto a bag of Nik Naks, saying nothing, but there was no girl child tonight. Julia looked at the small figure tucked between the wheels carefully; they had a bad history between them.

It would have been possible for her to turn the other way, walk the long way home and avoid the café door where the woman sat quietly holding a small bowl in her lap. In the light coming through the café

77

windows, it was hard to tell what, if anything, was in the bowl – a few small silver coins, a pile of money-rubbish, two- and five-cent pieces.

"Are you avoiding me, Julia?" the woman asked.

Julia pulled herself together. "Yes." She walked over to the wheelchair. "Yes, I'm thinking about avoiding you. Hallo, Lottie. You're out late, today. When are you going home?"

Lottie tugged at her shawl, and gazed at Julia impassively. "I'll go home," she answered. "I've got a way to go yet." Her fingers moved through the low heap of coins. "Jamela started day school. She needs shoes. They cost forty-nine rand at PEP Stores." There was no request in her tone, she was stating a fact.

Julia sighed, and sat down on the pavement next to the wheelchair. "Okay, then, there obviously isn't any avoiding to be done. I was going to go home to finish some work, but maybe, if you're here, we should try and fix things. If you're staying for another hour, or so. Do you want coffee while we talk?"

Lottie shrugged. "You broke the things," she said. "Now you want to fix them. Your rules. I'm not the one with the legs here. Four sugars, please."

"Four?" said Julia. "That's excessive. There's not enough room in the cup for four sugars and the coffee and the milk."

Julia walked into the café. At that hour of the evening it was only a quarter full and the man behind the till was reading something beneath the counter, chewing on his lip.

She had no idea how Lottie had got outside of that particular café door, the woman was ubiquitous. How was it possible for a woman, who weighed no more than forty kilograms, a woman trapped in a wheelchair, a woman who needed help to even go to the toilet, to travel across half a city, to show up on pavements and street corners, at the entrance to shopping malls and cinemas? She had a sudden image of Lottie, wheelchair tucked under her arm, racing through the city streets on long legs, folding herself back into the chair seat at exactly the moment she, Julia, came doltishly around the corner, un-suspecting, white slow.

She spooned the four sugars slowly into the polystyrene cup. (Why was polystyrene still allowed? Who did the allowing? Who could make for not-allowing? Someone. They. Them.) She put, sneakily, an extra cup around Lottie's cup so that it would be easier to hold, and went back outside.

Lottie was in the middle of a conversation with someone. He was a very fat pink gentleman, leaning over the wheelchair like an enor-mous polony, breathing into Lottie's face. He was saying, "The Lord gives and the Lord takes away, my dear; He gives and He takes away. Hmm. Yes. We must never think we know His plan. A plan He has for each one of us, my dear, for each one. Hmm."

His sentences ended on a little squeak, a shrill throat-clearing "hmmm-hmmm".

Lottie didn't appear too disturbed. She nodded. "It's true," she an-swered. "He has a plan. My Jamela, she is in school from last week, and the Lord, I know He is watching her. I know He will find her some shoes. I know He will not let us down."

The pink man reared backwards. "Hmm, my dear," he murmured, "the lilies in the field. And I say unto you, walk, and he walked. Yes, He has a plan."

With that, he gave the wheelchair a slight push, and strode off towards a sleek silver Mercedes.

"Oh, for heaven's sake," said Julia, steadying the wheelchair, and carefully placing the coffee into Lottie's hands. "Did he give you anything? What an oink."

Lottie took a long sip at the polystyrene lip. "The Lord does have a plan," she nodded, "but I don't know what he meant about lilies."

"Lottie," began Julia, "I'm happy to give you the money for Jamela's shoes. I've got forty-nine rand, even, with me. But we need to talk."

Lottie was silent. The words, *It wasn't me who stopped talking, Julia,* floated above her head, and sank beside Julia inside their bubble. They both looked at the swimming letters a bit askance.

"It's going to be one of those discussions." Julia shook her head resignedly. "I wish they wouldn't happen. I never know whether the bubble stuff is supposed to be me, or you, or whoever. Can't you just talk normally with me?"

"I *am* talking normally," replied Lottie. "Why did you get so angry, Julia? You were the one who treated me like I was a rubbish, like you didn't want to speak with me any more."

"I didn't think you were a rubbish, Lottie. I never thought you were a rubbish. There's nothing rubbish about you. But you broke our contract."

As far as Julia was concerned, the contract between them had been explicit. Julia would give Lottie a good portion of her rent money every month, sometime in the first week of the month. For her part, Lottie would not ask Julia for other things, would not phone her at home, would not send messages through friends to request special assistance for emergencies.

From the very beginning, it had been a contract designed to suit Julia. The frailty of Lottie's body, the stillness of her legs, had bothered Julia profoundly. The fact that she sat day after day, immobilised, exposed, seen and never seen, had prompted Julia to panic. She wanted to offer something predictable, ordinary.

And, a bubble enclosed a wavy sentence, suspended just above the grey of the pavement, casting an odd-coloured shadow around Lottie's feet, *Julia likes to be able to leave*. Lottie giggled as the bubble bounced gently against the wheels of her chair.

Julia felt furious. She tried to stamp on the bubble, as though it were a party balloon, but her boot just slid out from under her.

"Well, it's true," she said angrily. "I asked you not to phone me, not to phone my children, my lover, and you paid no attention at all. Sometimes you phoned six times a day, telling me to meet you at this garage, that street corner, that your grandfather had died, your cousin was at the police station, your husband – who was obviously full of crap from the beginning – had taken your money. You cried, and begged, and you even got Jamela to phone a couple of times. And every time you did it, I got upset, and asked you not to, to just stick with our arrangement about the rent."

"Asked is putting it mildly," remarked Lottie, taking the last gulp of her coffee and holding the cup out to Julia, to put in the nearby blue garbage bin. "You really yelled, you said: 'Lottie, I hate this! I just hate this!'"

Hate this! Hate this! Two lime-green word sacs swept upwards into the streetlight, whirling and jigging. One of them got snagged on the lampcover, popped with an alien hiss, and minute lime-green shards spattered down, flecking Julia's hair and the coat of a passing-by Golden Retriever (whose owner did not notice). The smell of the sliverwords was powerful – nausea, garlic, and bite all together.

"Gross!" Julia jumped to her feet, shaking her head. "That is revolting. Okay, I should have been calmer, I should not have yelled at you. I'm really sorry, I was even sorry at the time, and kept hoping you'd phone back so I could make things right, I knew I'd done wrong. But I did hate it, Lottie. I felt like you weren't listening to me. Like I was just some kind of soft applebody you'd suck at, with some new story of this happened or that happened, until I was pulp, you never took 'no' for an answer. You were like a leech in those moments."

"A *leech*?" Lottie's eyes opened very wide, and one hand gripped the arm of the wheelchair. "You thought I was like a *leech*?"

A pink bubble came to rest in front of Julia's face: *You have just called a poor woman in a wheelchair a leech.*

82

Julia blew into the words, causing them to get a little wispy.

"To tell you the truth, Julia," said Lottie, after a while, "I said thank you many times, but stuff happens. The Lord has plans. My grand-father did die. It was horrible. And my cousin was arrested for noth-ing, and we know nobody who can do bail, just like that, a Sunday night. And Jamela's shoes need to be on her feet. Where does a con-tract come in all this? I asked you. I found out where you stayed, where you worked, and I asked you."

Julia imagined embryonic sentences about homes, boundaries, the private, inside new bubbles, but they aborted themselves in the face of Lottie's reality: no private in a wheelchair outside a café, no bound-aries either, except the thick brutal line between garbage and human.

The small bubble that did appear, nothing to do with her, had a golden colour and it was hard to see the words inside. They spun out: *Motho ke motho ba batho babang*.

"I can't read that," said Lottie. "It's upside down."

Julia looked at her. "It's the usual," she replied. "A person is a person because of other people. I think it's misspelled. The words are about you, Lottie. They don't like me, they don't like who I am in this story."

Lottie gave her mouth a little twist. "I'm not surprised." She shook her head. "It's hard to like you in this story, Julia. You're ridiculous. But I've lost your phone number, so I won't be phoning you. I'm not going away, though. This conversation is going to continue."

Julia fished around in her jacket pockets for the money, and put it carefully into Lottie's bowl.

"Maybe tuck it away," Lottie said. "It's not so safe sitting there in the bowl like that."

Julia folded up the notes, and pushed them gently inside Lottie's shawl. "I don't know, Lottie," she complained. "I'm not one of those TV people – on call in the emergency room, sewing up stab wounds, making jokes, having an affair at the same time. No one's ever going to give me one of those awards for being an unsung heroine in my community. Maybe I need to eat more breakfast. Maybe my skin doesn't work."

"Or maybe it does." Lottie stared at her. "Maybe it works all too well, Julia. Whatever. I appreciate the money for the shoes. Jamela's been going in her old-old tackies, with the toes cut off the top, so her feet can fit in. The other kids laugh at her, but after tomorrow, they won't."

"Are you going home soon?" Julia felt at a loss, as though she was in a cul-de-sac, nowhere to go.

"Mmm," said Lottie. "My crap husband is going to come and get me at eight. This shop closes at nine, but it's too late to be going home after nine, and he is sleepy, he wants to go to bed."

Julia imagined Lottie, being pushed along the dark roads by the husband, chair tipped onto the back wheels so as to go faster, Lottie's face to the stars and clouds, the occasional word bubble bobbing above the pair of them: *How much? Tired. Ghosts and shades. Tomorrow.*

As she turned to go herself, the street ahead looked lonely; she knew no word would follow her home.

Michael

Her name was Michael. Over several years of wryness and office tedium, she began to trust me. This is the story she told me one evening, when I'd asked her about her relationships.

"I know it sounds stupid, but I am the woman who, when in love for the first time ten years ago, walked along believing only ancient Greek poetry gave me any glimpse of a precursor. I was a fervent would-be Marxist at the time, despising any suggestion of trans-historicism, so I found this link with a dead language disconcerting. Not disconcerting enough to destroy the growth of a creature I can only call a theology. I want not to call it theology. I want to say that, viscerally, I knew that women in our bodies are shatteringly precious, each one un-graspably precious. I have a faith in women's resistances to death, her resistance to what was death to/in her."

She was talking of her lover. Who had left her, not gently. And it's not my fault that she spoke the way she did – long sentences, so full of highfalutin philosophy and speculation. She was working something out.

"I remember learning about the depth of one woman from a photograph. I was sixteen, and I saw a newspaper photograph of a boy, his mouth gasping, his arms lugging the body of a thin, head-tipped-back child. He was running in a street of dust. Figures swarmed behind him – police, dogs, schoolchildren. The boy was wearing a filthy, bloodied shirt. The child was shot dead. And he was carrying the body into the camera, like a judgement. A girl was running beside the two of them, her mouth open in horror, running forever. I held the newspaper in my fingers all day without being able to speak. That girl burned into me.

"When I told this story many years later to a group of antiviolence activists, one said, 'Michael, it was a photograph!'

"She meant that I was a white girl, distanced by newsprint and technology from both agony and epiphany. But I knew I was a white girl; the sepulchre of my race was wound exactly, tight as piano wire, into the possibility of vision from a photograph. The point was that – at last – I had travelled far enough away from the crucible of the house into which I was born to begin returning home. My body had opened wide enough to let light illustrate the salience of one presence. One girl's running presence.

"What I was learning about was women, and this was difficult, not only because there were simply so many of them, not one really resembling any other, but because the endeavour made me feel like an eleven-year-old boy. Problems of quantity, or even the arrangement of quantity, I was up to; problems of impotence were volatile and deadly.

"Women were, then, so beautiful I couldn't bear it. I couldn't bear the ones who wore bright wraps around their temples, who yelled and whispered in languages I half understood. I couldn't bear the ones who stood like hunters in meetings: tense, hidden, bodies curled round doorjambs. I couldn't bear the young ones, running with cloth flying around their brown legs, giggling and on their way elsewhere. Especially, I couldn't bear the ones in expensive dresses, the ones who put their arms around men, any men – tall men, bronze men, red men, men with necks lapping over their collars, men with loud laughs and beers in whichever hand they weren't lending the woman.

"Years later, an organisation in which I worked as a drug counsellor held an emergency meeting to which I was explicitly uninvited. One of the issues on the agenda was, 'What shall we do? I think Michael hates men . . .'

"They decided that what was wrong with me was a slippery tongue rather than misanthropy, and I was advised merely to watch my assumptions.

"I don't hate men, but I came pretty close to it in those early days when I knew, like the eleven-year-old boy, that the women would never want me.

"The thing about being an eleven-year-old boy – probably the only thing that gets them through this room of raw misery – is that you can become a twenty-year-old man, akin, maybe, to the man against whose arm she presses. Elderly teenage women do not have this option. The fear of incompetence, of being looked through on the way to a body you can neither wait for nor want, the way it seems as though a man can make you evaporate, these might be reasons to hate men. Not, though, enough."

I wonder why she talks about not hating men, when actually what she is supposed to be telling me about – in that overwrought prose of hers – is loving women.

She drank whisky, and began to talk of herself in the third person. I once did that, in front of a psychiatrist. It was a mistake. And when Michael started doing it, I wondered where the "I" had gone, and why.

"One evening, in the sight of a mountain, in between a rugby field and a short underground tunnel, Michael was attacked. She was walking home when this happened, carrying a pile of blue-green examination booklets, which contained one hundred and twenty-four answers to the instruction: '*To the Lighthouse* is more about art than life. Discuss.'

"She was wearing a denim skirt. The skirt was too long and the combination of curtailing her fury at the idea of reading essays comparing 'art' to 'life' and preventing her boots from stepping on the hemline deafened Michael (and perhaps fatigue; or the green dusk air in the peace of suburbs which always propelled her into dissociation, quiet trances of obsession and argument). She didn't hear the shuffle and tread of fourteen feet; she heard a hand.

"The hand grasped her from behind her shoulder. It tucked itself into her clavicle like a crab, and made her jerk backwards. Michael twisted round, enraged, and saw a group of boys – nineteen/twenty-year-old boys – much too close. One, with dark eyes and a huge hole in the arm of his sweater, was clutching her shoulder and breathing at her – Scotch, cigarette smoke – and saying, 'Ja, meisietjie, dis nou nag, ja? Wat het jou ma van die nag gesê? Meisietjies moenie in die nag gaan speel nie; 'n meisie in die nag is soos 'n koekie wat wag.'

"There was no negotiation, no gap into which she could have spoken or spat. Time, in fact, spun itself out into a deep, pale pause, a century, during which Michael's head lay sideways on the tarmac, her left leg crunched up beneath her, her right twisting and kicking against gravel and feather-grass.

"They had thrown the skirt over her face, so it was through dark blue thread that she saw them as their faces came and went, changed and came back, like constellations auguring the lives of kings. None of them looked at her. They looked at each other. One in a red coat squatted next to her neck and tugged up her shirt, pulled out her left breast, pulled it away from her ribs, and threatened to slice it off with something Michael couldn't see – its blade lay thin and cold against her skin. Another one said, 'Ag nee, man. Moenie. The sight of blood. Nee, man, kak.'

"The pain in her vagina was making her choke, but they rammed on and on and on. She felt no liquid or blood or rips, she felt the slamming up through her colon into her mouth, she felt the sticky breath of their panting on the skin of her stomach, she felt her spine thudded onto the ground, against the heel of her boot, over and over again. And, not so far away, she heard a woman calling a dog, 'Kêrel! Come along, puppy! Mummy's waiting.'

"She thought a lot of things. She thought very, very fast, too fast for words, fast like the speed of light, leaving ghosts alone of what might once have been planets or words. Her thoughts streaked and spun away from the crushed lump of her limbs; she remembered an evening when she had gone swimming, naked, in the sea with a man called Peter. When she had scampered back onto the beach, chilled and bright wet, Peter had climbed on top of her. She had lain her head back and watched a forest fire racing, jagged and silent, along the mountain ridges behind them. She had said nothing. She had hated it, and lay passive as meat underneath his eagernesses. The fire was yellow and fierce in the sky; the line of dark mountain-wall and glinting swords etched like a carving into her eyelids.

"As the boys swapped and grunted, falling like enormous, obscene bags of pulp against her hipbones, the fossil line relit its edges into her eyes, and she thought about serration and skin. Michael knew hers was being scraped off, and without it, no embrace would be warm enough to stop her from dying.

"At the end of the century, still through the denim, her jaw locked so tightly she had no more lips, Michael felt, rather than saw, the low swing of headlights trained along the tarmac. The boy stabbing away at her arched backwards onto his feet, and yelled, 'Fok, julle! Gougou – die naai is mos klaar, bokkies.'

"The others lunged upwards from their positions sprawled across her arms, hips, across each others' jeans. One of them slapped her face through the skirt-cloth as he got up, and said, 'Dankie, poesie. My naam is Boetie-Bok. I know you won't be forgetting die Bok in a hurry.'

"She heard their feet stumbling away into a place from which they could never have come. Because they couldn't have been there.

"The car went some other way. Michael stayed on the road for another two centuries, pulled her skirt down over her hips as she, dimly, felt blood creeping out of her vagina. She didn't mind blood – the idea of a pool was quite nice.

"It was another dog (perhaps not another dog) whose barking, some time later, reminded her of the examination books.

"It took a long time to find them. All. It wasn't that they were badly scattered; it was that she couldn't count. She didn't know when she had one hundred and twenty-four.

"After a while, she thought, Fuck it, I have to get home.

"I have no idea how Michael walked home."

In the last line, she changed back into the right pronoun for herself. I felt so re-lieved. I've listened to quite a number of stories about raping, and it's critical to watch the pronouns. If the storyteller keeps moving her location, you have no idea who is really talking to you, and if you want to love her, that matters.

But then she changed back again.

"She did.

"The interesting part of that story, I think, is Michael's ferocity about the exam books. In retrospect, she probably couldn't imagine leaving snippets of Virginia Woolf's 'art' or 'life' in the dark, alone, after they'd had to lie, splattered and splayed, around her for three hundred years.

"After the loss of my skin, I was no longer a woman who read po-etry. I decided to become a mathematician.

"While the knowledge of violence grew in my flesh from an embryo of rhythm – two beats almost one – into full-blooded language, I resigned from my job as a teacher of 'art' and 'life', and began to spend my time in a library I'd never visited before, experimenting with books written for first-year university students about coefficients and calculus.

"The experiments involved measuring my brain against the texts' formalities; the promise was that if, by the end of each day, I had understood one new idea, if I could follow, faithfully and without demur, one new line of calculation, then being skinless didn't entail losing my mind. The library was high-ceilinged, and very still. At night,

I lay on my bed, whispering, repeating the day's formulae, as though each x, each sine or cosine, formed a knot on a rope with which I could haul myself, a thin hunk of reddened muscle, scribbled veins and cracked bones, through the urge to sleep. Without skin, you stick to things. Sheets, paper, dust. Sleep sucks you into the stick; getting up from the bedclothes means tearing small slabs of your self off cotton, looking at the rust-blood body print beneath the blankets. Just lying left imprints; something about sleep allowed the body its shadow as a rubbing.

"My days were hallucinogenic; streetlamps terrified me, and I spent a lot of time tucked up inside my wooden office cupboard, hearing the footsteps of people who wanted to see me click up to the closed door, waver, and click away to vanishing. In the early evenings, I took to frantic politicking in support of the growing resistance movement against a State which would have liked to ban the zebra, but it was politicking of the worst kind – manic, dogmatic, evasive. Every morning rushed me, starving and iron-white.

"Despite the memories of what living in a body could mean, the ferocity of Michael's passion for women didn't diminish. Alongside behaviour anyone watching would have coded incomprehensible, alongside lies of defence, lies of confusion and lies of plain defeat, this passion steeled itself into a civil war."

She has changed back into the third person – Michael has – just as she starts talking again about loving women. Why? I don't understand why.

"The war in her blood involved language. It was a war about language in which touch was the subtext – a granite heartbeat of inquiry and rage. The stakes of the war were bodies, women's bodies: hers, her mother's, the bodies of hungry women emaciated in the State's harsh unsighted glare, the bodies of angry women, the bodies of women bullying other women – pushing, shoving, not telling the truth. As it turned out, this war had been in her blood long before the boys had skinned her. It was ancient. Generations lived inside her and they all knew the landscape, only I learned (late) that the boys' attack simply accelerated the terms of the battle.

"I want to explain more.

"As I sank into the mud of my days, there was one very clear shelf beneath which I could see nothing and feel everything. What I felt was soft as fur, sad, immeasurably old. Above the ledge, words swarmed with ever-increasing complexity as they spiralled up towards the roof of my mouth.

"The words were often hollow and the earlier they were, the less they resembled things. The earliest ones drifted next to the ledge, like transparent skeletal leaves, just frail twists of air and stick. As they rose, some reeked of absence; others were like strange shells calcified over their fissures, forming fantastic beads. Where they whirled themselves into strings, they were like electricity, so fluid they bore no relation to my body. The silver flow of sentences was simply a last-ditch attempt to disguise the way the words were mostly fraudulent, and all at war with one another. Merely a double beat, she realised

94

that her heart's pulse was the effect of the axe whose swing had split her mind so that pain lived below the ledge and attempts at 'language' lived above. That rhythm was the ground from which those earliest leaf-words tried to reach up to catch someone's attention.

"Her determination to own a language of women's skin became ferocious; to own and to return it to the babies, girls, bodies – all walking round, freezing, sticking to things – to women somewhere refusing the coats of domesticity, irrelevance.

"By the time I encountered my lover (the one who left), in a different country, Michael was a woman. I was made of war, love, evasion, language, fur and arithmetic. I cut her hair and let cheekbones sharpen her eyes."

She smiled at me as she said this, and I saw how immensely attractive she could be, but I thought she was also irresponsible, someone who probably could not own her violence. I was shocked by the story of the gang rape, and was not sure that I understood her theories about language. Secretly, I didn't blame the lover for leaving. How can you stay with someone so sure of her own theories? Would she ever be able to just get on with the shopping? Walk the dog? Would she ever be able to account for her own slipperiness?

If I am to be the next lover I can see I am going to have to understand this thing about pronouns – where she actually is, how many of her there are, which one is hiding something, which one is the poet.

Or perhaps, I will simply love her.

She, me.

Virtual reality

Her friend had an enormous television set, broodingly present in the room, ruling the roost. On the day of the inauguration, she had begged a space in the lounge to watch the changing of a guard so dramatic that the entire planet demanded a seat in the audience. Some, a few, got to climb on aeroplanes and fight for an actual seat, or standing spot, to bear witness, but most homebodies looked for a TV set.

Her friend's house was already full when she arrived. Children were running and tumbling around the small garden, a toddler in a nappy with a huge smile was wobbling around and assorted adults were piled onto the sofa, the desk and anything else that would function as a chair, all leaning hungrily into the TV. She sat down on the carpet, very close to the screen, with her back to most of the others, scrunching a tissue between her fingers. The room went tjoepstil as things began.

A woman.

"It is my great pleasure to announce the president of the Republic of South Africa, Mr Nelson Rolihlahla Mandela."

A pause.

"Your majesties, your royal highnesses, distinguished guests, comrades and friends.

"Today all of us do by our presence here and by our celebrations in other parts of our country and the world confer glory and hope to newborn liberty. Out of the experience of an extraordinary human disaster that lasted too long must be born a society of which all humanity will be proud. Our actual daily deeds as ordinary South Africans must produce an actual South African reality that will reinforce humanity's belief in justice, strengthen its confidence in the nobility of the human soul . . ."

As the entire room sobbed and whooped around her, she sent him a message: *Hallo, hallo, do you remember me?*

He was clearly deeply immersed in his speech, his whole body solemn and formal, and he gave no sign that he had heard her. She did not, however, feel deterred.

Nine years later, the television was still her medium for contact. It was now possible to use a cellphone to send the old man a birthday message and along the bottom of the screen, for a whole day, messages poured in from the nation's homes like water: *Enkosi Tata, siyabonga. Hallo Mr Mandela, happy birthday, from the whole Jantjies family. Happy birthday Madiba, all love, Esme. Madiba, you have saved us, stay healthy and live long, Thivhilaeli and Agnes.*

She did not have a cellphone, but borrowed one from a friend sitting next to her on the couch: *They say u were constructed, they say we dreamed u, plse SMS back, ps, happy birthday.*

She hoped he would know it was from her.

There was no doubt that conducting a relationship through a television had its limitations. Firstly, there were already so many other people – always several in the screen, demonstrably several beyond it: pointing, moving, angling, arranging, cutting away and in, generally showing off. Secondly, she had no control over where things began and where they ended; contact could last for three minutes, an hour (interrupted by advertisements) or even ten seconds – a sliver of a sentence, a forbidding expression, an American model being embraced. Thirdly, and most difficult, it was impossible to tell whether he knew she was there.

Over the years, she had tried different angles to the screen (not always the same screen), and worn a range of garments designed to attract attention (a bright green kaftan, pyjamas decorated with flying pigs), but there was never any clear indication that he had noticed her.

She would wait for an appropriate moment – when an interviewer was surreptitiously looking at notes, or he himself was sitting listening to someone else at a podium – to assure him she was still watching. Once, he had turned his face in a way that brought his eyes closer, and she felt recognised, but on another occasion, he had moved his whole body with those long legs completely away, almost so that his back was turned, and she had spent the rest of the evening feeling blue.

There were particular moments when she would have been grateful for an acknowledgement from him, a slight tipping of the head or a glance outward towards the camera. She had returned, for example, from visiting a friend one evening, and spent the next twenty hours in front of her TV set, waiting to communicate. Her friend's story had been rough, and in the three hours of their conversation, accompanied by wine and numerous phone calls from other voices, had gotten rougher.

The outline was simple enough: her friend, Sandi, was a prosecutor in one of the special courts set up for "victims" (policy language) of sexual assault in the city. The court had been initiated, with much fanfare as a political ploy, by a member of the party that had not supported the African National Congress, and some of her co-activists had been wary as a result. Sandi, however, had surged forward. "We can make it ours," she suggested. "Who cares where the motivation comes from? We need this!"

Within a very short time, no adult women were being accommodated by the new court; all its services were requisitioned into meeting the demands of processing cases which involved children (legally anyone under seventeen). Sandi was a prosecutor, a short skinny woman with a temper and little patience for bureaucratic mess. She was not the best person for the job, perhaps, but pushed herself mercilessly to make good the stated promise of the court.

Sandi's latest case had driven her, literally, to drink. She had downed an entire bottle of red wine while explaining her sense of futility and anger. The case had begun with the sworn testimony of seven girls against a shopkeeper in their poverty-soaked neighbourhood. He was a lanky bespectacled man who made a living from selling a mêlée of goods in a run-down store – jeans, T-shirts, cassettes, clocks, cheap saucepans and other cookware, batteries and cigarettes.

According to the girls, the man had attacked them, taking them into the back of the shop, promising to show them special "goods". After locking the door, he put his hand over their faces, pulled up their skirts, fondled and pinched, and, in four cases, pushed his penis into their bodies, whispering that when it was over he would give them something from the shop, anything, they could choose.

However, not all of the testimonies patterned together. In one, the girl spoke about two men in the back of the shop and a threat to kill her. In another, one girl said that she was one of two girls taken and locked up together, but the other girl she named denied it and dismissed her as a "dumb malletjiekop".

Nonetheless, Sandi was convinced that the shopkeeper was a raping rat, and had poured resources into preparing the girls for the trial.

Two days before the trial was set to start (after a postponement), Sandi had received a message from one of the girls' mothers: *Anna has changed her mind, she doesn't want to be in the courtroom.*

100

Sandi had understood completely. Anna was a tense thirteen-year-old who twisted her hair into knots while she tried to speak; pre-trial jitters were natural. She drove out to the streets of dirty pink-painted apartment blocks and spoke to Anna – jammed into her mother's ancient couch like a barnacle – for two hours, trying to tell her how brave she was being.

Nothing, however, went right. The girls, despite the long hours of preparation, found being in the courtroom impossible. They giggled in weird places, struck poses, told the magistrate things they had never told Sandi, including (from three of them, all below fifteen) that the shopkeeper, who stood smirking at the table opposite Sandi, was a "nice ou", that he hadn't hurt them, that they had agreed to let him touch them for the "geskenke" and that, no, they weren't angry with him, they didn't want him to go to prison, bad things happen to men in prison. One of the girls, not Anna, told the magistrate that it was Sandi who had explained to her that what the man had done was wrong. She was only fourteen, but her sister had run away from home with her boyfriend at fifteen, and the shopkeeper had only talked to her about sex, he had not really put it inside her that much.

"Everything went pear-shaped." Sandi spread out her hands dejectedly. "It was chaos in there."

She wondered about pears, which seemed to her to have quite an elegant shape, fat-bottomed and smooth, but she understood the problem. The upshot had been the dismissal of the case. The shopkeeper returned to his store, reprimanded, a suspended sentence (re-lationships with underage girls) and the covert right to continue to offer jeans for sex.

Sandi had plunged into pitch-grey despair. What she said, cupping her palms around the wine glass, was, "So, we have a crime called rape, but we have no crime called poverty. No one goes to jail for causing poverty. You can go to jail for raping a teenager, but you don't go to jail for giving the teenager clothes when she gets no clothes, and will never get those clothes unless she bargains, and she'll bargain. It's not a crime. She's thirteen, but it's not a crime. If she says he raped her, that's a crime . . ."

The whole narrative hadn't made complete sense to her – surely there was still enough evidence of statutory rape? Why did it matter if the girls' tales didn't jive (seven girls, seven tales)? If the jeans were offered afterwards, how come that erased a before?

Sandi's distress, however, was so disturbing that she went home and begged her own TV to put her into contact. She needed a con-versation about why everything had gone wrong. Why – when you finally got a prosecutor who believed the witness, a safe story, where the perpetrator was not a family member/was an adult/diddled with almost-children, not one witness but seven (all identifying one man as the problem) – why then didn't the show come out with the right ending? What had she missed?

There was no sign of him that night, although she trawled through hours of news and political talk-shops, and even waited for the social conscience advertisements (occasionally, he could be glimpsed talking slowly and seriously about sex education). The next evening, she did find him: he was there in a gigantic, poorly executed painting dominating the lounge of a woman character, Faat Kiné, in the most recent movie by Ousmane. The movie was wonderful, she was thrilled, but the painting didn't work for her. He was too far removed, and there was no hope of getting through.

* * *

A week or so later she went to see a play.

In the play, a broomstick attacked a loaf of bread savagely and without mercy. When the broomstick was done, the bread lay scattered on the stage floor, bits mixed into a pile of sand standing there, other hunks jagged and illogical.

The broomstick had started off as a broomstick. It had been lifted high in the air, bristles to the heavens, and brought crashing down onto the three-year-old body of a boy who had wet his pants – the assailant was his frustrated, exhausted mother. The murderous broomstick was smashed into pieces, two splinter-ended bits of wood, which had then metamorphosised into the boy himself – broken, the bits lifted and cradled together for healing, laid carefully, carefully onto a sickbed. Later on, the broomstick attacked back, brutal as a missile.

The bread had also been offered an opening role as itself. Well, itself sort of. It appeared in a scene where the narrator was talking about being a thirteen-year-old boy, allowed to have a go with a "loose panty" woman in the settlement. If the boy (who had paid) couldn't finish in the time allotted, he got to ejaculate instead into a neat half-loaf of bread, sitting there waiting. The narrator had confided that he had actually preferred the bread, because the sound of the loose panty woman turning the pages of her comic was off-putting. So, the bread began as half-bread, half-loose panty woman.

Later on in the play, the bread had another role – although, as it still looked like a loaf of bread, the aura of the loose panty woman hovered. The new role was as a baby, wrapped in transparent thin-thin plastic. The baby-bread was rocked by a mother and then tucked into the statue arms of a figure of Mary – a strange angular carving, very like a small house god.

In the play, the mother who rocked the baby-bread had lost her own baby. Not actually, but actually enough for her to be represented in perpetual anguish, not speaking, waiting for her baby to return from the hospital perhaps, or from some foster home, too far away to be even imagined. Her own baby had been raped, and the last role played by the loaf was that of the little girl. Nine months old, said the theatre programme. Nine months old, had read the news-paper headlines. This was a true story.

While she sat and watched the broomstick destroy the loaf, the man sitting next to her giggled. He giggled quite a lot, for the full four minutes the broomstick took to finish. At the first giggle, she wanted to jam her elbow backwards into his stomach, but as he didn't stop, she wondered whether he was simply too young to cope.

As far as she was concerned, not coping with the broomstick's behaviour was probably a sign of sanity. She went home and stared for a long time at the broom beside her own fridge. It looked domesticated. She thought of the phrase a character in the play had used to describe the sight of the abandoned baby, "red cauliflower", and felt too sick to sleep.

And where was he? Did he even exist?

The TV screen was giving nothing away. He could have been anywhere – in China, holding hands with Hillary Clinton. He could be tired. She had watched a TV interview in which a fierce housekeeper woman had insisted that he be allowed to leave the conversation early enough to prepare for bed at a decent hour. Decent meant nine o'clock, it seemed.

"Why do you think that talking to him would make any difference?" her friend said in an exasperated tone. "He wouldn't even like you, you know. You are hopelessly undisciplined, you hate doing what you're told; he gets up and does exercises at five-thirty in the morning. He would think you were a sloth. And if he saw those sheep slippers you insist on wearing, he would never believe you hold down a responsible job."

"It's true," she said sadly. "I even hope for tax refunds."

"There you are," her friend said, nodding. "You want a tax refund. He gives his money to children's charities. You are slippery with the facts; he is honour personified. You two have nothing in common, and if I were you, I would stop mooning over the hope of contact because the day he did actually speak to you, your socks would get pulled up so hard you'd probably choke."

"Mmmm . . ." She lapsed into silence, imagining herself strangled by her own socks.

At the age of twelve, not unacquainted with broomsticks, she had been (she thought) asleep in the double-storey house in which her parents lived. Of at least one of her parents she was afraid – a fear masked by mockery during the day. Her bedroom looked out onto a balcony, with a low white wall and a green railing.

As she lay on the bed, she had seen a parent stealing across the balcony, searching – she knew – for her. She had flattened herself into the sheet, her ribs becoming backbone, a mere slice of body. Her eyes had stayed fixed on the window, watching the figure creep past in the dark, hunched over.

As the danger moved off the balcony, another quite different shape tiptoed past, his face turned towards hers. As he slid past the window, tracking the parent, he winked.

His face was young, bearded, and she had never before seen it, but she had known it was him, grasped that he knew what her parents were up to. All she had to do was keep the secret that he was shadowing their every move. It was over for them.

She said nothing of the dream to her friend.

How do you know what's real? He looked solid enough in the TV, when the air force ripped through the sky above his head. The baby who inspired the story of the bread and the broomstick had not been born then, but many others had. She could still see that wink in her mind's eye, deliberate, conspiratorial. She picked up the remote, began scrolling through the channels.

That he'd been made up? It was not possible.

Taking the initiative

1

Do you remember the poems? I kept them for years, almost in defi-
ance of you and your decisions, the decisions that were the dark.
For years now, too, in the dark, I am no closer to full comprehen-
sion and wonder what such poor vision must have meant for you.
Perhaps it is exactly this, my poor vision, which told you in which
direction you needed to walk.

Do you want to know what I remember?

2

Memory, these days for me, is like a stomach and I have an eating disorder. Everything is swallowed, but nothing gets digested. Images of space, weeks of conversation, detail upon detail upon detail, crowd inside my body until there is no more room, not one corner. Maybe it's true that you are what you eat. Me, I am the places and the women I remember. I am re-membered by their being my body and, in acquiescence, the sodden, complex, unstable earth of my mind. As firmament, fundament, I am interested in nothing else. I am obsessed, swimming, touching again and again the words and moments with them through which I've been born.

Theologically, my only hope is that I've been right all along – that this quest among women's singularities, their skins, their deep, incredibly deep thought, is taken on in the name of god. If I'm wrong, I am up shit creek. And not the shit of some sweet, tetchy dyke either, no, the toxic viscous shit of the man. The man. Shit that his body refused, can you imagine?

You will not approve of my language. You will think of your husband (of whom I am not talking, because you can do that for yourself), or you will point out to me that men come in different races, different classes and that I am a white creature. But I wasn't talking about the shit of men. Just the shit of the man: the one who said to you that you weren't beautiful. The one who tried to finger my vagina while his wife was in the next room. The one who couldn't remember the woman's name and refused to take her – Thandi (Love) was her name – to the hospital at two am, her body twisted, bloody through miscarriage, because (he actually explained) the blood would damage his car seats.

3

In a piece called "The Miracle of Black Poetry in America" June Jordan asks a question about Phyllis Wheatley's eighteenth-century writing. "Was it a nice day?" she asks, in Boston, 1761, when John and Susanna Wheatley washed their faces and drove off to the market to buy a new slave. They called her Phyllis, as though they could, and, asks Jordan, "Was it a nice day?"

How could there be day, let alone weather?

But, in Cape Town, 1981, the streets were filling with bullets, and schoolchildren ran into one another's yards, plotting and strategising like the commanders they were. There were helicopters in the sky and buses on fire and weather every day as people were dragged into the back of police vans, their testicles crushed, their mouths gashed open. I could not become acclimatised to the corrosive air, the smell of what needed to die, and would not. The Island, savage and near, winked at the white sunbathers on Clifton's beaches, and it is true that I was continually surprised, surprised until fucking stunned.

You, however, in the middle of the salt wind, which carried the smell of Rolihlahla's comrades' sweat from the Island's quarries, you did not surprise.

All those years ago, you lay on my raggedy blue-green carpet with the frayed edges climbing up the walls – "For the cats to play with," I said, but really, my scissors were not strong enough to trim the edges down to the room's size.

Your arms were above your head and your sweater was angora, and crimson, plum crimson, and you said, "Do you know what you're doing?", as I put my palm over your left breast.

And I said, "Yes." Which was true.

4

You were angry after I'd left. You didn't tell me, but others did. You were particularly angry about the poems; felt that I'd taken something that belonged to you away so far you'd never get them back.

The story I told, in those years, when I had to have a story to tell, became very simple. I could give it in a dozen seconds. "The first (you know). She was married when I met her. At first she was going to leave her husband. But then she didn't. Which was a good idea for her, but a terrible one for me. And then she went to live in another country, married someone else, had a son; we lost touch."

The first therapist believed I was really heterosexual, but such myopia aside, she was gentle. The second wrote me a poem herself about the kind of journey I would have to travel between nights spent on the San Francisco docks (screaming at container-ship workers who unloaded crate after crate of South African citrus) and the nights spent alone in my shack, too thin for the warmth of the struggle.

You get a message to me, a pastiche message, because even though you know it will get through, you won't sign it. It's a cross message: "You must take the initiative."

I am still surprised by this country's hallucinogenic days. The years' geographical distance has done nothing to immunise my stomach against the relentless state stupidities old and new, the starvation, the occasional devastatingly bizarre epiphany about alignment. I wait and listen, attentively. I carry an umbrella – black and gold and green (old-fashioned, now, and worse, can you believe that?) in the fierce mountain winds – and use its point to jab the stomachs of men, at memorial rallies for organisations. I am, on the whole, quiet.

But here is one response to your message.

I did already.

Take the initiative.

It was an initiative gauche and dented and truly astounding because I (like you) was brought up in a world where the truths of the Zimbabwean bush were edited into examinations on English daffodil poems, where comic book women and men made the love of Wilbur Smith – illicit, and completely divorced from the daily skirmish of father and mother, mother and men who were servants, mother and Esther (Esther whom my father would never look in the eye).

I took the initiative so far away that you wouldn't follow. You said it no longer had anything to do with you. I took the initiative and I have never stopped. I can't come backwards; the journey forward developed my muscles, taught me to breathe underwater for so long that I now know, exactly, the intolerability of "air" – the weather normal around us all.

Was it a nice day?

These days, a national museum houses an Island exhibition – cell sizes, in feet and inches, are listed; photographs of uniformed guards stare out of their metal frames.

Where it counts, I no longer have days, which makes me happy and lonely, anguished and mainly lucky. I am so lucky. Not to have been surprised by you. I was so lucky then, all those years ago; the time in which I live now, you gave.

Given initiative, initiation, I have not yet stopped.

I think I have a long way yet to go. Every day I learn how little I know of a compass. I learnt yesterday how to creep down Silvermine in the dark, following the course of rain rivers thick and foam-white. When I looked up through the wet leaves, a banana-moon hung in the sky, sharp and yellow. Her light glanced across the slippery stones where I was perched, not afraid, not either at home.

This is an invitation.

Whodunnit

1

The moment she opened her windows, looked up and outwards to the city weather, she knew what had to be done. She should have guessed something like this would occur, but it still took her breath away. She shook her head roughly, in the hope that she'd made it up. Nothing changed. It was still there. Across the whole sky. There couldn't be a single person in the city, from Site B to Princess Drive, who hadn't seen it.

It was a painting – not oil, or watercolour, but something else, with a shine and brilliance she'd never seen. The images seemed to flow between dimensions – two here, three over there. The interlock of layer and tint compelled like the eyes of a snake, and yet if you stood still, kept gazing, something melted and reassurance began to seep down your oesophagus into your hipbones.

The painting was an extraordinary piece of work. As Zuzi stared, incredulous, she had to acknowledge that she was probably looking at the finest white art in nine centuries, but as a fact, this was of no comfort whatsoever.

The painting's central image reminded Zuzi of a photographic negative – the lines refusing shadow, hinting gently at the macabre. What one discerned was, however, unmistakable. A woman's body, naked, covered with trails of blood, desire, hopefulness, lay half-curled, half-sprawled along something green and gold. Above the woman's eyes, which opened themselves out with the longing for sex, for touch, there was another body. It was hard to tell the gender or the colour of the second body. Tall and strong, the figure strode away across the painting's horizon, so beautiful in its tenacity, its impatience.

It was clear that the relation between the humiliated body and the one which soared was one of brutal necessity. Exposure had released invulnerability, someone in shame gave someone else feet of steel, and the colours of the exchange lit the city sky like a diver's lamp in the deepest sea.

There was no signature to the painting, but Zuzi would have known Agatha's work in her sleep.

She felt sick and, clutching at her dressing gown, turned back into the bedroom only to meet the eyes of the woman, spread out over the sky, in her closet mirror. The same pale skin, the same dipped waist, the woman in the sky was portrait-exact: Zuzi-in-reverse. Zuzi.

The whole thing had to be stopped. Imagine trying to get a job, a taxi, a washer fixed, when one's photograph was stuck up – in great art – all over the horizon. Zuzi figured she'd be recognised in half a second by the guy selling newspapers, the one with the jokes and the black bags on the corner, all her students, her cat and the eleven members of the book club. Im-fucking-possible.

She attempted solving the first immediate problem by tying a yellow scarf around her head, and pulled from the back of the closet clothes she hadn't worn for years – a dress with frills down the bodice, a pair of brown sandals. She scraped blotches of caked eye shadow into small palettes of purple and crimson, and did her best to become someone she wouldn't recognise, someone whose body was not in love, all over the sky.

The second immediate problem was sky-wash. There must be some way of erasing the wretched artwork, even if the sky itself were to be a little damaged.

As her stunned mind stumbled into gear, more and more options buzzed in Zuzi's brain: perhaps the painting violated some municipal law? Or maybe it could be termed pornography, and no one would be allowed to write about it, or attempt to get it preserved? Or perhaps it *should* be preserved? As quickly as possible taken out of the sky, and tucked away into some cultural museum for expert study, some museum almost no one had permission to enter. Surely works of such value shouldn't be allowed to just sit there, getting stained by the smoke from thousands of informal settlement fires? Wasn't it dangerous to the city's welfare – distracting to taxi drivers, alienating to people who didn't like art, making life difficult for meteorologists?

Zuzi began to perk up. There was no way the painting was going to survive more than twenty-four hours. In three days, nobody would even remember it.

It wasn't until she pushed open the cold glass doors of her flat block, the early winter wind whipping at her ears and mouth, that Zuzi saw the futility of her schemes. She wanted to cry. If Agatha could paint one picture like that, in under ten hours, taking over the entire sky . . . If Agatha could capture the blindness of that body, abandoned, stalled in the knot of neurosis called passion, what was to stop her from doing it again? Why should anything prevent her from rehearsing that image, over and over, in every medium? There was no doubt that such images would sell. Like wild cherries, like liquid gold in plastic, they'd become currency themselves.

Zuzi thought of Agatha's head. She imagined banging it against a wall to shake free the other pictures of Zuzi, the pictures of Agatha herself, pictures of surf, pictures of tickets. She wondered why it mattered that the painting lied, and was magnificent. Could paintings lie? If she, Zuzi, knew something else, why did it matter that Agatha's Zuzi-in-the-sky looked like Zuzi's own nightmares of herself? Were nightmares lies?

The wind was tugging at her scarf; Zuzi paid no attention. A sanitation truck pushed and hooted all the way along the street, but she didn't hear it. A man with two skinny Afghans mincing on leashes down the opposite pavement stopped and stared at her. He shouted, "Yo! Hey, you! Aren't you the lady in the picture?"

Zuzi gawked as one of the Afghans peed against a tree.

"Nice tits!" the man continued. "Do you really want it that bad? You can have my number any time."

2

Agatha's sudden death made newspaper headlines, mostly because of the place in which her body was found.

It was found sitting, bolt upright, hands folded into the black cloth of her smooth dress pants, in one of the upstairs seats at the Baxter Concert Hall. There was no sign of violence: her black briefcase lay neatly under the seat, her face was still, her head turned sharply away from the stage, her hair neatly swept up over her forehead, smelling of lemon.

A man pushing a huge yellow vacuum cleaner through the stone nooks and corridors of the concert hall had come across the body. From across the atrium, he'd thought it was an early morning visitor, some eccentric dignitary with special permission to tour the hall when it was officially closed. It wasn't until he'd approached the row, rather deferentially, and asked at Agatha's spine, "Excuse me, ma'am, are you visiting here? I just need to finish up this side . . .", that the peculiar quietude of the body disturbed him.

3

"Your Honour," said the grey-haired woman standing before the bench, "this is no ordinary inquest. There is no reason to suspect foul play in the death of Doctor M, and yet there is every reason.

"Doctor M was fifty-one when she died. She was the youngest member of the National Arts Academy, the youngest and from what I've been told one of the most important. Her last piece sold to a gentleman from Arizona for seventy-five thousand American dollars.

"She was found dead on the morning of the 31st. It has been ascertained that the hour of death was somewhere between nine the previous evening and midnight. The body shows no signs of injury and the medical examiners cannot establish cause of death. Although I have no immediate suspicions about how or why this happened, I have no reason to think that Doctor M's death was planned and therefore every reason. I am requesting the case remain open until my offices have had time to pursue a full inquiry."

"What did you mean?" a reporter asked the woman outside the hearing afterwards. "What did you mean when you said you had every reason to think someone planned to kill Doctor M? Was she someone other than Doctor M? What were you talking about?"

The woman looked straight through him, and elbowed her way down the courthouse stairs. For someone of sixty-plus, she moved like a raft, a sharp little raft rushing through the rapids of lawyers, hangers-on, court security and the doleful lines of people trying to get in, or out, of the building. Her fingers were long, nails short; hands ready for work.

Her name was Yasmyn Naidoo. She had worked with the prosecutor's office for decades, and only one person in all the years she'd come in and out of those brass-handled doors knew that Yasmyn Naidoo went home to Saluuh Molokomme's iron-strong arms, soft-shell mouth, her fake Thai cooking (Saluuh was born in Botswana) and her giggle as Yasmyn slipped fingers inside Saluuh's skirt – the same giggle for twenty-two years and the sound still made Yasmyn wet.

"Not as wet as we once were," she mumbled into Saluuh's knotted hair, reaching with her free hand into the little jar on the kitchen shelf and rubbing the lotion against her own busy fingers under Saluuh's skirt.

Watching Yasmyn Naidoo manoeuvre herself into the messy city streets, the reporter thumped his own way down the steps in a huff. It was only his third week as a court reporter, and it was clear he'd missed something about the Doctor M story. Yasmyn "the crone" Naidoo had suspicions and she never fucked around, but there was no evidence, no witness, not even a stupid cause o' death. He didn't, come to think of it, even know why Agatha was called Doctor, a Doctor of what?

4

To: Doctor Agatha M:

*I find your conduct beyond description. You did not respond to my
letter of the 2nd, despite my explicit request that you do so. When
I finally reached you at your offices (I called countless times, to be
informed that you were "at the studio", "in conference", "unavailable"),
you failed to recognise my voice, misremembered my request
and finally subjected me to several minutes of your mirth. You then
dismissed me by saying that you had important work to do, and could
no longer continue our conversation. Doctor M, I warn you that
this kind of response is not characteristic of those I work with. Should
you continue to count yourself amongst these, consequences will be
both immediate and dire. Should you ignore this letter, do not be
surprised by a disgrace to which demise may be preferable. I can be
contacted at 084 746 863.*

Samuel Jenkins

Yasmyn raised her eyebrows, slipped the letter inside a manila folder,
and continued to pick through Agatha's office. Alongside the missive
of Mr Jenkins, she had some tax documents, letters from colleagues
about research and references, letters from an attorney about the sale
of something called "Hips Dive", a note from someone which read,
"A, I'm sorry, I was upset, it just doesn't make any sense to me. Love

Z" and messages to call back Dr H, Frances, Juanita, Xolisa, The Gallery.

As she walked out of the office, she ran her finger along a painting on the wall – one of Agatha's earliest. The finger fell into liquid, the painting sliding up her wrist, bathing her hand in light – blue, crimson. It felt like being in a humming bath. Carefully she drew back her arm and the colours glided back into the frame. A sentence appeared along the wall: *WAS THAT GOOD FOR YOU?*

TOO?

Yasmyn knew she should laugh, but something stopped her.

Yasmyn Naidoo put on her glasses and opened the top portfolio on her desk. An assistant had scurried around collecting copies of Agatha's work, all the way back to 1993 when her first opening – thirty paintings of hands, all of which seemed to reach out of their canvas to touch, tweak, beckon, slap, pinch – called "Palm Reader" had galvanised national, even international, attention. Now Yasmyn, no lover of art, was faced by a fat pile of catalogues, magazines, folders, one or two books on who was who and what was what in the art zones of the new century. She wasn't entirely sure what she was looking for.

She turned one, *Surfing,* upside down so that the image of the surfer slamming head first into the coil of the wave looked like a woman with a halo. She ran her hands across it, but the copies didn't carry the extraordinary effects of the originals.

There was a whole series, a recent one, in which the same figure appeared – a woman with huge eyes and pale skin, always in a version of deshabille: a breast sliding out of a shirt, a pair of not-quite-crossed legs that revealed glistening labia. The figure was sometimes grotesque, sometimes beautiful, but she had no sense of self-preservation, and this ruined a sexuality. One could shudder, laugh, masturbate, but one could not avoid the figure's angles, the conviction of her own innocence at terrible raw odds with every colour around her body, every colour within her body.

There was one painting where the figure, clasped by a round, dark-skinned man on a dance floor, was keen-leaning towards Yasmyn at her desk in a way that made her think she should be hit. The title of the painting upset her: *All She Needs is a Good Fuck*.

Much too close to her own reactions about hitting.

Yasmyn poured over the delicate, contorted white woman for a while. She couldn't describe the feeling the painting aroused in her, but it was not comfortable. Finally, she made a call to Samuel Jenkins.

6

"Tar and burning oil," said Samuel Jenkins. "Evisceration."

He picked up a tea pot, ringed with gilt around its belly, poured tea into a cup and handed it to Yasmyn.

They were seated in Jenkins's study, surrounded by photo portraits of a hundred faces – brushed hair, salve on the lips (for shine), their open eyes looked trustfully out of the wallpaper. Yasmyn had made no secret of her status, nor of the reason for her visit; she had even brought a colleague, requesting that he be allowed to sit in on the discussion.

"I was not surprised by her death," he went on. "A little regretful, perhaps – she was not old and it is possible that she may yet have matured into someone more, how shall I put it, aesthetically balanced. As it was," his shoulder pads lifted a little, "I'm not surprised except by what seems to have been the peacefulness of it all. Tar and boiling oil would not – in the eyes of some – have been inappropriate. Evisceration. She was a dangerous woman, you know. One can't go about in the way she did and expect the infinite patience of the Divine. No, indeed."

"I believe you are an artist of some stature yourself, Mr Jenkins," Yasmyn said, mimicking his syntax. "You must have had occasion to meet Dr M personally?"

Her colleague snuff-giggled into his Kleenex. Careful, thought Yasmyn. The letter was in her colleague's briefcase, but Yasmyn had not yet opened the manila folder for him to read its contents.

"Ah . . ." He pressed his fingertips together. "Yes and no is the correct response to that. Yes, I did indeed meet Dr M. She is a trifle ubiquitous in this city; her opinions about cameras, about what photography is and is not. Yes, I met her often and, might I add, always to my discomfort. And, no, I did not meet Dr M. On the single occasion we were to meet face to face, at my request, she was not in fact there. We did not meet."

"You mean she missed the appointment?" Yasmyn asked.

"She missed the appointment. Yes, indeed," replied Samuel Jenkins, as he refilled his own teacup, "she missed the appointment."

"Let me ask you a question which you may find offensive," Yasmyn went on, switching abruptly back into her own rhythms. "I'm sorry, but it's necessary. What were you doing on the night of December 14th? What do you remember?"

Her interlocutor didn't start or raise his eyebrows; instead he reached behind him to grasp a thick notebook. "Let me discover," he said. "This is my appointment book. A little full that time of year – I am in great demand for Christmas life studies, you know."

He drew his finger down a page covered with black flourishes.

"On the night of the 14th, I was at the home of the Mathabanes. A charming family. The father has done quite beautifully here, quite beautifully. One of the new order, you know. It only takes a little hard work. And beautiful English, beautiful. They were sending a life study to grandparents, in Lusikisiki, I believe. In fact, one of the pieces is behind you." He pointed.

Yasmyn turned her head: five children, heads grouped together like a bunch of flowers, ten brown eyes liquid and smiling. Beside the Mathabane family was a photo portrait of another family. The longer one looked, the harder it was to tell the families apart.

Yasmyn felt a little queasy. Firmly, she asked for the Mathabane's address and phone number. Then she opened the briefcase and handed Samuel Jenkins the folder.

"What can you tell me about this letter?" she asked mildly.

7

Yellow scarf notwithstanding, after the remark by the man with the Afghans, Zuzi had retreated to her flat for the rest of the day. The phone rang frequently, but she didn't even allow the answering machine to pick up the calls. She drew the blinds, screening the image of her own eyes out of her bedroom and sat like a refugee in front of her television set, waiting for the noon news.

When it finally appeared, she had to sit through President Bush in the DRC, floods in India and the city mayor in a tiff with municipal workers protesting outside her office, before, accompanied by shots of dozens of women and men gazing fervently up at the sky (which looked on the TV screen exactly like ordinary South African sky), the newscaster said: "Cape Town awoke this morning to something unusual. A painting in the sky, covering the whole horizon."

Yea, verily, thought Zuzi.

"We have been assured by the city's Health Department that the painting is not in any way dangerous. Its only peculiarity is that it cannot be photographed. So we can't show you it on your television screen. What we can show you are the artists from all corners of the city, and beyond, who have poured out to make copies of the painting. Tune in again at five o'clock for our interview with some of these artists and we'll show you their work."

The newscaster gave a skew smile and then her face changed to a more suitable expression as she began to outline proposals for toll increases on the newly opened scenic driveway around the coastline.

Zuzi picked up the phone and called Agatha's number. Her answering machine responded brusquely. "Agatha," said Zuzi, trying to speak like a person, "it's me. Give me a call when you can – I'm at home."

The effort at normality failed because, in two minutes, there was Agatha's voice – on Zuzi's machine, "Zuzi? Zuzi? Pick up . . ."

Zuzi held the phone very carefully, like a pillow next to her collarbone. "Agatha. Listen, nothing's the matter, but I have a question."

"You're lying," said Agatha. "I know you . . ."

"It's the painting," said Zuzi.

Agatha laughed. "I knew you'd know," she said. "I was going to phone you. Do you like it? Tell me everything."

"Darling," said Zuzi, very carefully. "Darling, are you going to let people know it's you? Don't you think they'll figure it out?"

"That's not your question," said Agatha. "I did it last night. I didn't even know I was going to. I was stunned myself. What do you think? You don't like it?" Agatha's tone quavered: a fifth outrage, three fifths pride, one fifth fear.

"Agatha, the woman in that painting, to me, that image looks like me. When I look in the mirror, I see the same shape, only in the mirror my body isn't doing what she's up to in the sky. Now, I want to know why you did that? If you did it?"

"What do you mean?" asked Agatha, withdrawing. "If I did it?"

"I know you did the painting," she said. "My question is about verisimilitude. A man recognised me from the painting this morning and harassed me."

There was a long silence.

"Agatha," said Zuzi.

Agatha's voice returned, sounding old, wounded with information. "I don't really want to have this conversation," she said, "but you don't sound so good, so . . . I think you should ask other people who've seen the painting about that image. Are you so sure it looks like you? Maybe it was looking like you when the man saw you?"

Zuzi knew she was out of her league.

"The image doesn't look like you to me – that's not what it's about," said Agatha. "Why can't you see that? You're not being very smart about this. You are being egocentric. I'm interested in what you're do- ing, but, yes, it is egocentric. If you see your body in the sky painting, that's got nothing to do with me. I was actually thinking about my father when I did that painting. It's about my father."

Agatha's father had been murdered when she was a teenager. He'd been a revolutionary, a man of great discipline and some sweetness, but there had also been something odd in Agatha's relationship with him, something unresolved, something subterranean. Agatha rarely spoke of him, but he was evoked everywhere in her choice of gurus, the lies she told her brothers, her religion and love of boxing.

Zuzi peeked through the blind, but the painting was still there and the woman's body still resembled the one in her mirror. She felt puz- zled – it was clear she hadn't understood something.

Agatha was still speaking, ". . . so I'll call in a couple of days . . . things are pretty busy around here . . . I'm going to hang up now . . . Zuzi? . . . Zuzi, aren't you going to say goodbye?"

Zuzi said, "Agatha?"

But Agatha had already put down the phone.

8

It turned out to be a good thing that Yasmyn had brought along a colleague on the Samuel Jenkins excursion.

At the sight of the pages clipped together inside Yasmyn's manila folder, Mr Jenkins's teacup began to skip upon its saucer and his left knee gave a spasmodic jerk.

With immense difficulty, bobbing and nodding his head, he swallowed and attempted to sit the dancing teacup back onto the table. The cup chattered and hopped itself frantically onto the floor at Yasmyn's feet – smashing off the little white handle, spilling pale tea everywhere. Yasmyn brushed a few droplets off the folder and perhaps it was the movement of her fingers that tore away Samuel Jenkins's last wisp of composure.

With a peacock yowl, he flung himself at Yasmyn, clutching and scraping at the air. "Give me the letter, the letter's mine," he sputtered. "You silly bitch! What do you people know about art?"

His wild leap happened so fast that it took Yasmyn's colleague half a second to spring at Jenkins's flailing torso, hurling him away from Yasmyn and the folder, the contents of which were now spattered over the whole room – lying in puddles of tea, fluttering against the blinds.

"Get off me, you lout," screamed Jenkins, kicking like an ostrich. "Get your filthy hands away from me. Why don't you go get that woman? Why don't you brutalise her? She's the one you want, her and her filthy women, her deviants, her art," his sneer was unbelievable, "her filthy, crawling, lying art. She took the whole sky, the whole of God's sky for her filthiness. She deserved evisceration."

Yasmyn's colleague grunted and yanked Samuel Jenkins's arms behind his spine.

Yasmyn herself, not really too shaken, walked round the furious wriggling body and squatted down in front of Jenkins's face, his nose buried in the pile of the carpet.

"Okay, Mr Jenkins," she said. "What do you want to tell us about Agatha M? What did she do to you?"

But Samuel Jenkins just collapsed into the carpet, refusing to speak. It was in fact five years until he began to speak again and even then, in a long-term psychiatric hospital, all he could say involved imprecations against postmodernism.

* * *

After the ambulance had carted away the mute body, Yasmyn and her colleague wiped up the puddles, collected the fragments of china and searched the apartment thoroughly. Not entirely to Yasmyn's surprise, they found one whole room stuffed with information on Agatha: hundreds of photographs, clearly taken from awkward angles or from behind trees – Agatha walking, Agatha at work, Agatha with different people (in restaurants, on the pavement, looking in shop windows). Press clippings about her paintings, and boxes full of articles she'd written or others had written about her, annotated in fibrous green ink; spiders of vitriol whipping up and down the margins. There were also large charts, or perhaps timetables, with an X marked here and there, and sometimes a word – "sighted", "unchanging".

The whole room stank of camphor and sweat and Yasmyn's eyes quickly began to sting. She carried the piles of paper and grime into the hallway, and poured over the photographs for a couple of minutes. Something was itching at her brain.

It was the same woman.

The pale woman she'd stared at in Agatha's paintings, the one with sensuality and pain written all over her skin. It was her face in Jenkins's tatty spy photographs, here standing beside Agatha in a cinema line, here dimly glimpsed through a window on a street above Green Point.

Yasmyn was feeling dizzy. As she sank back on her heels, her colleague emerged from the Agatha archive, holding a canvas at arm's length.

"Looks like the old geezer could paint," he said. "Remember when that painting happened and people copied it? The painting that turned into coloured dust and rained. God, it was so beautiful . . ."

Yasmyn stared at the canvas. She did remember the sky painting. It was hard not to remember it, even with a fresh news scandal every twenty minutes. She took the canvas gingerly from her colleague.

It was that woman again.

And even through Samuel Jenkins's bad copy, a hint of the sky painting's panache, its violence and passion, whispered excitedly against the frame.

9

She was smaller than Yasmyn had expected, and a huge black cat wound itself around her ankles as she opened the door.

"Sorry," said Zuzi, as the cat sniffed the hem of Yasmyn's sari. "Do you hate cats?"

"Not at all," said Yasmyn. "She's beautiful."

"She's twenty-two years old," said Zuzi, proudly, picking up the animal as though the cat was a gigantic baby. "Would you like some tea?"

Although she suspected who her visitor was and why she was there, Zuzi felt astonishingly calm. She liked Yasmyn's face, and she liked the fact that she seemed quite unofficial (no colleague this time, Yasmyn had left him behind on purpose).

"I don't think so." Yasmyn had unfortunate memories of tea. "Maybe some water?"

As Zuzi went into the kitchen to find a glass of cold water, Yasmyn glanced around the flat. When she'd called Zuzi to request a meeting, there'd been no surprise in Zuzi's voice, no surprise and no alarm. The emotion she'd heard was something different, something without defence.

When Zuzi returned, she handed Yasmyn the glass and sat down. "Do you ask me questions?" she said. "Or do I talk? I've never done this before."

Yasmyn smiled. "You sound like someone in a therapist's office," she said.

Zuzi gave a grimace and giggled. "I suppose it doesn't feel that different to me," she said. "Anything to do with Agatha makes me feel like I need an analyst, and you told me on the phone you wanted to talk about Agatha M."

"I do want to ask about what you knew of Agatha M, but this isn't an interrogation, and you don't even have to talk to me if you don't want to. Discussion with people who knew someone who died in mysterious circumstances is usually handled by other members of my office, but Agatha's case seems complex to me, and I'm doing some of the preliminary work myself. I just know that you were a friend of hers . . ."

Zuzi's head was bent, and as she raised it, Yasmyn realised she was trying not to cry. "How do you even know that?" she asked.

"It's a long story." Yasmyn's voice was careful. "In the end it involves some photographs brought to our office's attention. Photographs of Agatha. Seems as though she had paparazzi. So we have pictures of some of her companions, and you're one of them, that's all. Identifying you wasn't hard. You've been arrested quite a few times, you know, over the years . . . Governments change, but national records have long memories." She spoke gently.

Zuzi nodded, and sniffed. "I never figured on being identified as . . ."
There was silence.

"As . . .?" Yasmyn's voice steadied itself.

Zuzi was feeling exhausted. For the past week she'd been sitting in her flat all day, trying to read or write, scrubbing the floors like Lady

Macbeth. At night, she'd been walking along the seafront, up and down, striding past walls, fences, corner-shop windows lit and un-lit. At six or seven in the morning, she'd return to her flat, her mouth full of the taste of the night city – shadows, garbage, headlights, bread baking. She missed Agatha. When the phone rang, her arm leaped – almost out of its socket – to pick it up, in case Agatha was there, on the other end, wanting something. On hearing someone else's voice – "Zuzi? Is that you? You sound very odd . . ." – she'd mutter, "Wrong number, lady . . ." and hang up.

The only reason that she'd allowed herself to have a conversation with Yasmyn Naidoo was that she'd been asleep when the phone call began. Halfway through – "No, it's fine, you can come here, the ad-dress is . . ." – she'd awoken and all she could remember was that someone quite official knew Agatha and was coming over to talk about her.

"As me, I guess," Zuzi whispered, "as a me who knew Agatha."

Yasmyn waited.

"Because that wasn't the only me, you know. There were other Zuzis – one who went to meetings, one that goes to work and one that refuses to cook. But the real one was someone who talked with Agatha. Agatha was too much for me, you know. I guess you know how smart she was. I'm not smart like that. Did you ever go to one of her shows?"

"Mmm-hmmm," Yasmyn lied. "I've caught most of her work in one way or another."

"Yeah, well," Zuzi sniffed again and tried to smile, "some of it's pretty hard not to catch."

"Is that where you met her?" asked Yasmyn, tactful as a regent. "At an art show?"

Zuzi shook her head. "No, I met her . . . Well, it doesn't really matter where I met her, but I've known her for quite a while. From before she was having art shows. But I always knew she'd become famous, it was sort of inevitable, something inside her like an arrow, something sharp and fast. I always thought she'd be happy when she was really famous, but I think I was wrong . . ." Her voice trailed off.

"Agatha wasn't happy?" Yasmyn didn't usually operate like this – it was just like being a therapist, she thought, but the Zuzi woman looked brittle, ready to shatter at any moment.

"No," said Zuzi, suddenly animated. "No, she wasn't. Sometimes she even said she wasn't. She'd say, 'Zuzi, I'm not happy . . .' with surprise and distress, and it was like she was utterly confounded. And she wanted loyalty, she wanted everyone to love her and be loyal, and the more famous she became, it was as though she expected more people to like her, and protect her, and of course some did, but a lot more didn't. She always hated being attacked at conferences, or in art reviews. That was one of the reasons we never went anywhere important together – she never wanted anyone to attach her to anyone, or anything, and then have, you know, some way of hurting her."

Zuzi stopped, unaware of the amount of information she'd offered.

"So you were attached to her?" Yasmyn asked, reeling the small fish in very gently.

"Well. Oh shit . . ." Zuzi started. She was quiet for a moment. "Well, it's too late now, I suppose. I don't even know what you already know about Agatha."

Yasmyn noticed Zuzi's fingers twisting themselves into claws against each other. "I figured she was lesbian," she said, "but maybe that's wrong."

Zuzi used a napkin lying on the table to wipe her nose. "It was such a big deal to Agatha, you know. She wanted to be entirely in the closet. She didn't want anyone to know, but it was all over her work, and it was all over her life too, her private life, I mean. I wasn't the only one, there were others, but I stuck around. We had good times and terrible times, and sometimes I couldn't stand it any more, but I loved her, you know, or . . . I don't know.

"It was horrible in the end, because I knew she'd always leave me for some other woman and that she'd always return and expect me to be the same, and I always tried to be the same, and I always blew it. She wanted me to be invisible, she even said so, she was completely upfront about it, she wanted to be totally loved by me, and totally unaware of me, that was how she could be safe, she said. That was how she could keep on doing her work.

"I wasn't strong enough, in the end, to do that. I wanted her to talk back to me, but she wouldn't, she said it would ruin her art, and maybe even kill her . . ." Zuzi's sobs overtook her sentence.

Yasmyn wasn't sure she was understanding, but one thing was for sure, Zuzi was in a fine old mess, and it seemed as good a time as any to produce awkward questions.

"Tissue?" She handed Zuzi a tissue from inside her briefcase.

"I want you to have a look at these." She pulled out the gallery photographs of some of Agatha's more recent paintings. "Tell me something. I don't know very much about art, and I believe it's not fashionable to say that something in a modern painting looks like something else, but, to me, this figure, here, and this one," she pointed at the photographs, "they resemble you. What do you think? Am I reading something into them?"

It took Zuzi at least ten minutes to collect herself. Yasmyn had never seen anyone cry quite like that.

"You don't understand, do you?" Zuzi stared at Yasmyn, who shook her head, somewhat resignedly. "Well, you're gonna have to. I don't really know who the hell you are, but there's no way you can even think about Agatha if you don't understand where she was working from, what made her want to live and everything."

To Yasmyn's surprise, she took Yasmyn's hand in her own.

"You'll never get to the bottom of this if you don't understand. It's ideas, but most of everything is an idea, so that's not too weird. Agatha didn't believe in reciprocity, you see, she didn't believe, in the end, anything could be a direct exchange – that, say, she could draw a flower and then you would see that flower on the canvas. Instead, Agatha believed everything was vanishing, always on its way elsewhere – the flower, her painting hand, especially you looking at the painting. Especially. She didn't believe a figure, say that figure," Zuzi pointed at the picture of herself in the dancing man's arms, "could *be* me, or anything to do with me. Pictures weren't *of* anything, do you get it? Pictures escape, they transform, but they're never there as any kind of reality."

Yasmyn's hand was hurting a little, crammed between Zuzi's fingers, but she didn't want to take it away. Zuzi had stopped explaining and was looking into her face intently, watching for a flare, a raised eyebrow. Yasmyn said, "So. I think I've got it. Agatha didn't believe in reference. She didn't believe that if I say 'cow' I could mean something going 'moo'."

Zuzi beamed at Yasmyn, and gave her back her hand. "That's it," she said. "That is exactly it! Agatha didn't believe anything could be fixed, she didn't believe in the verb 'to be', and she thought people who do were morons, responsible for the ACDP."

"To be," said Yasmyn, thoughtfully. "So, no to be, only 'to pretend'."

"Or 'to guess'," said Zuzi, "'to play', 'to perform', 'to conjure'. Lots of verbs do the trick."

"When you saw these paintings," Yasmyn went on, "what did you think?"

Zuzi scrumpled up the tissue. "I had a fit," she said. "Not only because of the me in the picture, but because that actually happened. We went to a bar, and Agatha wouldn't dance with me, she danced with some man, and I had to, too, and it was silly, it was so wrong.

It was one of those nights where I really loved her. You know how it can get? We'd been together for years, you know, off and on, mostly off with an option for on, but still, you know, it was complicated. Then you just get those moments when you're in love with someone all over again, even though there's history, and rubbish everywhere, you just suddenly love them. It was like that.

"But she wasn't there, she was playing some game with the men in a Long Street bar, a reggae bar, and she wouldn't dance with me, and I didn't really know what was happening anyway. She told me she liked watching me, you know, when I was wanting her, and you know, that made me feel creepy and kind of dumb, and then, a couple of weeks later, there was the painting, with that title, and she was so proud of it, she was so happy . . ."

Yasmyn shuddered. "Did you talk to Agatha about it?" she asked.

"I tried," said Zuzi. "I was so embarrassed. The woman in that painting, she looks like, well, you can see what she looks like. And I thought, if that's what I look like when . . ." and her voice broke. "I did want her, it's true, but I didn't look like that . . . That's like a straight woman in a magazine being a spaniel pressed open by some man's boot, wanting to be a fucking spaniel in front of everyone. It gives me the creeps, and I dunno, how can I explain . . . I feel so ashamed, you know, it made me feel like dying."

"Shh," said Yasmyn, her own eyes beginning to prickle. "Shh. It's okay. It's okay. I know it's not like that."

"You do?" said Zuzi, gulping. "What do you know?"

Yasmyn thought carefully and then rested her fingers against Zu-zi's cheek. "I know it's okay to want. I know it's okay to want a woman. As much as you like. I know it's okay for a woman to want. I know that want is a pretty stunning thing. And I know it's between you and who you want it to be between; it's not an exhibition. That's what I know and I think that's what you're trying to explain to me. That being in love with Agatha didn't make your body ugly . . .? Yes? But then you had to look at her paintings and in the paintings, the woman in love is horrible; pathetic and obscene."

Zuzi leaned her head into Yasmyn's cheek. "It hurt so much. She did the work and I got to see my own nightmares. I had to sip wine in rooms full of people and make like it wasn't me, all bare and fucked up on the wall . . ."

Yasmyn had been a prosecutor all her life. She couldn't let it slip. "Zuzi, my dear," she said, her hand still against the wet cheek, "in the picture we're talking about, *All She Needs is a Good Fuck*, you're not bare, you're wearing red pants. You're thinking of something else, another painting. You're thinking of the sky painting."

The room fell very quiet.

"Did you see it?" asked Zuzi after a while.

"No," said Yasmyn. "I refused to see it, the whole idea annoyed me, and it made my lover mad, too. She was angry for days afterwards."

Zuzi tried to smile, noticing the disclosure. "So it had to stop," she said. "It couldn't go on. Can you imagine? The whole of the city staring at you like that? I don't think she even knew what she was going to paint before she painted it, I don't think any of it was malicious, but I had to do something. I had to stop her. I had to."

"How did you do it?" asked Yasmyn quietly.

10

Zuzi wasn't crying any more, she was sitting very still. "I didn't mean to kill her," she said. "She may not even . . . anyway. It was a camera. I did it with a camera."

Yasmyn waited for a second time.

"I knew a lot about Agatha's head, you see," Zuzi eventually said. "I knew about all her exchange stuff. I wanted to show her that something did exist, that it wasn't all disguise and going away." Zuzi's voice slowed. "I just called her name, I just called her softly: 'Agatha!'

"Her face was full of the orchestra and the light and she didn't see me because I was off to the side. What she saw was the flash of a camera, and no one holding it. She just saw the eye, the mechanical eye, but there was no one behind the lens.

The camera was balanced on the ledge behind her chair, I had set it up that afternoon, and then I'd just hung out until things started. I do that all the time, usually because I want to see the performance, and I can't afford it. Anyway, I pressed the shutter from where I was in the dark. Remote. The camera just took her. She went. She just went. Gone. Nothing to meet her. Just her and the machine. There was no one to catch her image, and, you know, fling her back into the world, give her a response so she could stay in her body, and you can't come back unless you know you're being watched. It took less than a second. I was stunned. She wasn't there, but her hair was shining in the stage lights. Ever since then, I've been crazy. I feel safe because she can't paint me any more, but I miss her, I miss her so much I can't think."

Yasmyn found herself speechless.

"So where is she?" she asked.

Zuzi pointed. A small, very ordinary camera, was sitting on the bookcase.

"I haven't exposed the film," she said. "I was going to, but then I couldn't. I don't know what I'm going to do. Are you going to arrest me?"

Yasmyn stood up slowly, and stretched. She walked over to the camera, and peered in through the lens. "Tell you what," she said, "why don't I take this . . .? No, not to a police station," she went on, answering Zuzi's face. "Can you imagine explaining this in a police station? We'd both end up in a psychiatric ward. No, I was thinking of something else. My lover, Saluuh, and I are going on vacation in a couple of weeks, and we could do with a camera. We'll take a few pictures and if Miss Agatha is ready to be developed, we'll see what happens."

Zuzi looked at Yasmyn Naidoo.

"And you," said Yasmyn, "you'd better get out of this flat and into someone's mouth. The twenty-first century's no time for slacking. Holes in the ozone layer, sulphur in the rain, even cats' life spans are three years shorter than they were a century ago. There're women out there waiting to be touched all night and then again before breakfast."

Yasmyn looked carefully at the camera, picked it up, and tucked it into her bag. She let herself out, and walked carefully out onto the street.

Against her will, her eyes travelled upwards, but the skyline was completely blue, stretched matt around the city bowl, a rim of silk.

Acknowledgements

Many people read *Porcupine*, or parts of the collection, as it grew. My thanks especially to the generous hearts and sharp eyes of Yaba Badoe, Gabeba Baderoon, Helen Bradford, Debbie Budlender, Maggie Davey, Ingrid de Kok, Dorothy Driver, Shereen Essof, Michel Friedman, Pregs Govender, Colleen Higgs, Desiree Lewis, Amina Mama, Jenny Radloff, Anne Schuster and Sally Swartz. Your gentle and not so gentle – *"Aren't you scared of what people will think of you after this?"* – feedback honed syntax, connections and resolve.

And nothing would be the same without:

Alison and Rebecca

The Saartjie Baartman Women's Centre

The Kalk Bay Book Club

Thank the goddess we're no longer voting . . .

JANE BENNETT is at an awkward age: old enough to know better and too young to understand the meaning of patience. She lives in her head, but pays visceral attention to what her heart tells her of the countries in which she lives, and of the women she is lucky enough to call her family. She is deeply attracted to language, as defence, as invitation, as conundrum.

She has worked as an activist, feminist, writer and teacher. Her home is in Kalk Bay, Cape Town. She has written extensively as an academic. This is her first publication as a fiction writer.